THE LUCKY DRAGON

The Lucky Dragon

a grown-up fairy tale

Samantha MacDonald Solberg
&
Beth MacDonald

The story quoted on page five is from the outer packaging of the Wedding Fantasy Barbie, copyright © 1989 Mattel Inc.

ISBN 979-8-9943052-0-1 (E-book)
ISBN 979-8-9943052-1-8 (Paperback)

Cover art and design by Romy Klessen.
Interior art and design by Beth MacDonald and Samantha MacDonald Solberg.

www.NorthInkBooks.com
Printed in the United States of America
First Printing

Advice from a fortune cookie:
Embrace the surprises that come your way.

PROLOGUE

A Long Time Ago

1982 ~ SALLY

"I knew you'd bring down the house! Once you win the Van Cliburn, there's gonna be no stopping you," Ben said as he looked with pride into Sally's eyes. "You'll play concert halls around the world, and I'll follow you—your husband, manager, and biggest fan."

"I really like the way you think. . . Someday. . . " Sally breathed deeply and stared at the cellophane wrapped rose adorned with baby's breath she held in her hands. Her thoughts were on Ben's words—*if only our future together could start tomorrow*. . . "The rose is really pretty," was all she said.

"It looked kinda puny next to some of those bouquets they brought out while everyone was clapping."

"Ehh, most of those were from people who want something from my parents—yours are the only flowers that mean anything to me."

"Someday I'll get you a dozen—no, make that two dozen—red roses."

As the young couple strolled hand in hand from the auditorium, their footfalls clattering on the granite floor of the now empty atrium, Ben stopped to pull an oversized advertising postcard from a display rack. Emblazoned with a photo captioned "Sara Johnson," the picture showed an attractive young woman standing beside a Steinway concert grand. The bold print on the card announced her as the grand prize winner of the Midwest Association of Piano Teachers' annual competition. 1982 was the first year that Sally had been old enough to compete in the top division. A solo concert backed by a professional orchestra, the performance that Sally had just given, was part of the grand prize.

"I love that picture—even my mom thought I finally looked thin enough—but I wish they would've called me Sally. I don't think of myself as Sara."

"You'd better get used to it—at least in the music world. Sara's classier than Sally—it has more gravitas," Ben responded.

"Aren't you fancy. 'Gravitas,' huh. I suppose with a name like Bentley B. Bradley, *the turd,* you'd know."

"The *third*, you turkey—and, yes, I do think my name has gravitas. It'll have even more once I graduate from law school and add 'Esquire' to it." Ben grabbed Sally by the waist and swung her around in the echoing atrium. She tightened her arms around his neck and collapsed onto his chest; Ben sank his face into Sally's soft brunette curls and kissed the top of her head.

Sally let out another sigh, shrugged, and shuddered. "I am so tired—but wired—like every muscle in my body is wound tight and twitching. Give me a hug?"

Ben pulled Sally even closer and wrapped her in his arms. She continued to clutch the rose and baby's breath bouquet to the back of his suit coat until he released her from his embrace.

"It's been such a perfect night—I don't ever want it to end," Sally said while looking deeply into Ben's eyes.

"I love you, Sally Johnson. I promise you, that will never end."

1989 ~ NORA

Nora sat cross-legged on her grandparents' beige wall-to-wall carpet, cradling a large box banded in bright pink and embossed with what looked like an overlay of white Chantilly lace. Through its heavy cellophane, she gazed wistfully at her new Wedding Fantasy Barbie.

"I wish your mom would let you play with the dolls we buy you," Gloria Wanamaker said to Nora.

"Oh, it's okay Grandma—I like having my special Barbies in boxes. Daddy built me shelves for my bedroom so I can look at them. Momma says someday—if I take care of 'em—all my fancy Barbies might pay for my college," Nora said, her voice tinged with resignation.

"Well, I don't know about that—but we'd better listen to your mother, hadn't we? Could you bring the box over to me so I can look at that pretty doll again?" Nora stood and carried the doll to her grandmother. "I had a bride doll when I was your age, but she was bigger than a Barbie." Nora's grandmother looked at the white clad doll through the cellophane and turned the box to look at the back of the packaging.

"Read me the words, Grandma. Please?" Nora said.

"Oh, it's probably just advertising. Let's see. . . Well, look at that, it's a story." Gloria began reading in a practiced story-telling voice:

> Wedding Fantasy Barbie is dreaming of her wedding day, and what a beautiful day it will be! There are flowers everywhere. Soft music fills the air. And Ken looks so handsome in his tux. As Barbie moves down the aisle, everyone turns. She is the most glamorous bride they've ever seen! Her spectacular gown covered with iridescent lacy roses in full bloom, sparkles in the candlelight. Her veil floats like a cloud around her. She is so happy. She knows that someday her dream really will come true.

"Do you think you could read that on your own?" Gloria asked.

"Not the big words—but most of it," Nora said. "Are there books about Barbie with pictures? Books I could read by myself?"

"I don't know, but you know who we can ask? The children's librarian when we go to the library tomorrow morning."

"Yay! I love your library, Grandma," Nora said. "Can you read me the box one more time?"

"Sure, honey. Come sit closer and we'll look at the words together." Nora sidled up to her grandmother on the living room couch. They began to read in unison: "Barbie is dreaming of her wedding day. . ."

ACT I

The Once Upon a Time

CHAPTER 1 ~ SALLY

September 12, 2018

Sally Munson sat on the edge of the bed and rubbed her face. Her eyeballs felt as though they'd been rolled in sand, her right leg ached where she'd broken it years earlier, and the bottoms of her feet hurt. *Unfair*—she hadn't even put any weight on them yet. *Weight. . .* why did she have to think about that unpleasant subject so early in the day? Sally hated her weight. She grabbed the apron of pudge that hung from one hidden hip bone to the other and gave it a squeeze. Beneath her knit cotton nightgown the roll of fat felt like the hefty mid-section of a boa constrictor that had recently enjoyed a bunny-sized lunch. The combination of two c-sections and menopause had snuck up on her like some sort of sick algebraic story problem:

> Sally is 52. She had her last baby, Tiffany, 15 years ago. The emergency c-section to birth her older daughter, Trudy, took place 20 years prior to Tiffany's birth. After Trudy was born, Sally had weighed 106 pounds. She'd gained an average of 10 pounds per year, but had lost an average of 7 pounds per year. How much did Sally weigh by the age of 47? Adding 25 pounds to Sally's weight at age 47 and subtracting the 2 pounds Sally had lost during Waist Whittlers sessions last year, how much weight is making the edge of Sally's bed sag this morning?

As far as Sally was concerned, *too darn much.* She dropped her midsection and ground her fists into her eyes, then stood, groaned, and hobbled down the stairs to make coffee.

What are the proportions? Bruce usually made the coffee, but he was in Moorhead for another sales meeting. *Six cups of water to three scoops of ground coffee*—she thought that's what he'd said every time she'd asked. She wasn't fussy. Well, maybe that was her problem—if she were pickier, perhaps she wouldn't eat and drink so much. She'd start watching her diet soon. . . *maybe tomorrow, maybe. . .*

Disrupting Sally's musings, Tiffany yelled from the top of the stairs, "Mom, where'd you put my jeans?"

"Have you checked your closet?"

"Duh—why'd you even ask?"

"Laundry?" Sally shouted as she opened the dishwasher.

"Didn't you do the wash yesterday?"

"I was busy." Sally began putting clean plates into an upper cupboard while looking at the un-rinsed stack of dirty cereal bowl, plate, and glass that Tiffany had left on the counter following her late night snacking. Sally shook her head.

"Mom, I really need those jeans. How could you not do the wash?"

"Actually, it was pretty easy. A lot easier than doing it—which you'd know if you ever did it." Sally said, her voice getting louder with each syllable.

"It's not my job," Tiffany yelled from the second floor.

Sally grabbed the silverware basket from the dishwasher and set it on the counter with more force than required. The clean knives, forks, and spoons bounced in the air and then dropped back to the basket. As Sally sorted out spoons for the utensil drawer, she pondered: *So, when did it all become mine? . . . When did everyone's problems become exclusively mine? I wish someone could tell me.* Sally raised her voice another notch and yelled, "If you're serious about wearing that pair, you're just going to have to wear them dirty."

"I can't—they're gross—I wore them Monday. They're the only ones that work with the shirt I'm wearing today. You ruin everything!"

Sally waited: three, two, one—BAM! The slamming of Tiff's bedroom door had been her argument encore since the day she'd turned twelve. Sally was used to it, and it didn't bother her nearly as much after she'd poster-puttied the lower corners of all the hanging pictures to the walls.

Sally walked to the laundry room. Tiffany's jeans were on the floor where she'd dropped them two days earlier. Sally lifted the stylishly hole-laden pants, checked the pockets, and shook them over the waste basket. *Not much fall-out,* she thought. As she gave them the sniff-test, she noticed a small pizza sauce stain on the left leg. She grab an old hand towel from the rag drawer, rinsed and wrung it out, then rubbed the spot clean. Sally threw the damp towel, jeans, and a fabric softener-sheet into the drier to tumble. *Good enough is good enough, especially when the pants in question look like they should be in the rag drawer.*

Tiffany sat at the counter eating toast she'd spackled with peanut butter. She wore a stretched out T-shirt and flannel shorts; with her left hand she scrolled her cell phone. She didn't bother to lift her head or speak when Sally walked through the door from the laundry room hallway.

"Tiff, make sure you're home from school early. Trudy's coming by to see us—says she's got some news."

"What if I have plans?" Tiffany said in a tone more belligerent than inquiring.

"Sorry—change them. Your sister's more important."

"Not to me. Besides, I saw her a few days ago. Is *Turdy* bringing the brats with her?" Tiffany took a bite of toast.

"She didn't say, but I suppose so. And, please, don't call her that," Sally said as she poured a glass of milk for her daughter.

"I'm just kidding, Mom—she knows that. Besides, you're the one who named her, not me."

"I named her Trudy, not *Turdy*. I thought it was cute. I never dreamt kids would twist it around so."

"What? Kids weren't mean when you were one? It must've been nice growing up in the Middle Ages," Tiffany said. She wiped her face with the clean dishtowel Sally had just set on the counter.

Sally grabbed the towel from Tiffany's hand and snorted, "Kids were mean then, too. I guess I just wasn't very imaginative. Your jeans are in the dryer—you'd better hurry, it's almost eight."

"I know what time it is. You don't have to keep telling me," Tiffany said and walked toward the stairs.

"Your jeans. Dryer!" Sally pointed toward the laundry room even though it was too late for Tiffany to see the gesture.

Tiffany called out as she bounded up the stairs, "Don't need them—I'm wearing something else."

"Of course you are. . ." Sally said under her breath. She stretched and shrugged her shoulders back creating a deep valley between her shoulder blades. She released the pose and raked her hands through her hair still styled by last night's pillow and perspiration. Her fingers hadn't helped the hairdo, but they hadn't harmed it either. *Another day in paradise. . .*

Sally dropped Tiffany a block from the high school. Heaven forbid Tiff's friends should see her mother driving her to school. Actually, Sally didn't mind allowing her daughter to walk the extra block, it let her avoid the critical mass of teens in cars streaming into the school's parking lot. Tiffany's reticence to claim Sally as her mother was an unintentional favor. *The only kind of favor Tiff is willing to grant me*, thought Sally as she rounded the corner to head toward home and the mountain range of laundry awaiting her. She hated laundry. Maybe she should go on strike—that'd show them. *Nah—I need clean clothes too.* She had so few that still fit, and her recent hot flashes caused those to get tossed into the hamper far too often. *Still*, she thought, *dirty clothes cannot be my whole raison d'être—they just can't be.*

Sally had been gainfully employed as a bookkeeper at a flooring company before the family had moved from South Dakota to Minneapolis to be closer to Trudy, Enrique, and the twins. It hadn't been a high paying position, but Sally had enjoyed working at the little startup and learned so much about building a business during the eight years she'd worked for Step Right Flooring. Now, however, with Trudy counting on Sally's help with the boys, paid work wasn't a priority. With Bruce doing so well and with the sizable trust she'd inherited from her mother's estate, the family didn't need the little bit she could earn at a clerical job. And, while she missed having paying work, and, as much as her youngest would protest that it wasn't true, Tiffany still needed her mom. In a year, when Tiff started driving, Sally had decided she'd look into the local job market. At least, until then, she had her thrift store work. It had been almost two weeks since she'd made her rounds—maybe it was time for some strategic thrift store shopping after she threw in the first load of laundry.

~

"Hey, Sally, how're things hanging," James called from behind the cash register as Sally walked into Second Chances, the hospice thrift store appropriately located on Second Avenue.

"Low and lower, James," said Sally as she comically glanced down at her torso. "Hey, but other than that, life's pretty good. Anything new?"

"You know it. We've been wondering when you'd be in."

"Yeah, I'm about a week late—been babysitting my older daughter's twin boys. I love 'em like crazy, but they're definitely a handful now that they're walking."

". . . I can only imagine," said the older man.

Sally grabbed a shopping cart and went straight to the clothing. Without looking at style or size, she threw all the green and yellow clothes—men's, women's, and children's—into the cart. She followed up in the linen aisle, gathering everything that was predominately green or yellow from that area as well. By the time Sally was finished, the little shop practically glowed red.

"That'll be $58.00," James said while he pushed the last of a pile of green and yellow shirts into the huge blue IKEA bag that Sally had set on the counter.

Sally pulled cash from her wallet. "Thanks, James . . . Say, is there anybody in back doing intake today? I've got some stuff to donate."

"Red stuff I bet." James said, counting Sally's payment into the register.

"Yup, you're on your game today," Sally said. She hefted the nearly full IKEA bag over her shoulder while expelling an audible groan.

"Tom's around back—he'll be happy to help you."

"He always is. See you next week." Sally pushed open the heavy glass door with her back and wrestled the awkwardly wide bag to the parking lot. She popped the back hatch of her Sportage where three more IKEA bags sat in a row. She sorted the green and yellow clothing and linens into the half-full bags by color, then grabbed a bag that contained only red items. She carried it around to the alley at the back of Second Chances and rang a doorbell beneath a sign stating: "RING TO MAKE DONATIONS—CLEAN ITEMS ONLY!"

"Hi, Tom."

"Hello, Sally. Got some red stuff for us?" Tom reached for the large blue bag and dumped the contents onto the table of donations he was sorting and pricing. He held the empty bag out to Sally.

Sally took the bag and began to noisily fold the stiff plastic. "You bet. Not as much as last time, but I think it'll pick up again as the weather gets cooler and people start going through their closets."

"Thanks for the donation. I know what you're gonna say, but do you want a receipt for your taxes?" Tom waved a photocopied form at Sally.

"The answer's still no."

"Figured, but I gotta ask—it's part of the job," Tom said as he shrugged one shoulder and gave Sally a 'whatcha-gonna-do-about-it' smile.

"That's fine. Enjoy your day, Tom." Sally turned to leave.

"You, too. Got any fun plans for the rest of the day?" Tom said to Sally's back.

Sally stopped at the door and turned toward Tom. "I've got a couple more thrift store stops, then a mountain of laundry to attack—just another day in paradise. . ."

As the heavy metal door closed behind her, Sally grimaced. . . *Ohhh no, did I actually say that out loud?*

CHAPTER 2 ~ NORA

September 12, 2018

Nora Wanamaker rolled over and grabbed her phone from the nightstand to turn off the alarm, nearly knocking her water glass to the floor. Steadying the glass, she sat up checking her phone for messages that had come in while she slept. Her alerts showed a few emails, including a wedding RSVP from her cousin Greg—regrets, thank God, she'd only invited him because her mother had insisted—and a couple Instagram likes on a photo of her and Brad from their engagement photo session that she'd re-shared the other day. The photo had been part of a series of posts serving as a countdown until their wedding: 45 more days to go! *ring emoji*

But there was no "good morning" text from Brad. That was okay. Her fiancé was a busy man. Training for a major marathon while planning a wedding and holding down an executive position at an advertising firm was a lot for one person to handle. He'd likely left for his run early and just forgotten to text her. He'd been forgetting more and more lately, but Nora decided that didn't matter—today was her big day. Today was the day she finally got to try on her wedding dress! She'd been waiting months for it to come in and she couldn't wait to don it and feel like a proper bride. Nothing could bring her down today.

Nora set down the phone and pushed back her duvet. The sun, already streaming through the filmy windows of her studio apartment, lit the place like a soundstage. She looked around and thought about how much she liked its creaky wood floors and crown molding. It had character. Plus, it was affordable. Soon she'd be moving into Brad's two-bedroom condo in a new high-rise downtown. While part of her would miss the simple life she'd led here for so many years, she had to admit she was looking forward to the new building's heated, underground parking ramp and on-site gym. Not that Nora ever went to the gym. . . But, maybe once she had a facility only a few floors below her, she'd start. Who knew what kind of person she'd be once she was Mrs. Bradley Baumann?

Nora swung her feet off the bed and sunk her toes into the cozy fake fur rug that made it bearable to emerge from her cocoon of blankets in the winter. It was still warm outside, but in a matter of weeks the thick fur would be welcome. The rug was zebra-striped, and Nora realized it would clash horribly with the vibe of Brad's cool blue bedroom. *Oh well, the condo has better heating anyway. I won't miss it.*

She padded to the bathroom and squinted at her reflection in the mirror. She needed to shower and wash her hair before the wedding dress appointment at 10:00. Her light brown hair was much longer than usual–well past her shoulders. She didn't mind that it was long, it just took so much longer to blow dry than it used to. She needed to factor in an extra ten minutes for that. And she should probably eat something for breakfast. Her mom always liked to remind her "coffee isn't breakfast." She also still needed to put on makeup—Nora was sure that her mom would want to take pictures of her in the dress.

I really should have set my alarm for earlier, Nora thought, as she popped in her contacts. But she'd been up late and hated the idea of an early alarm on her rare weekday morning off work. Last night, instead of going to sleep after her shift at the restaurant, she'd finished a library book that was due back today–*Where the Crawdads Sing.* One of her former grad school classmates had received an advanced reader copy and raved about it on Facebook, so she'd nabbed an early spot on the library waiting list. The book was great, but she was glad she could return it today after work. While she didn't want to get a late fee, more than anything she wanted to make sure that this copy could get passed along to the next person. There was little that pleased Nora more than sharing a good book with someone, even if that someone was just the next stranger on the waiting list.

As Nora brushed her teeth, she took a quick look at the banking app on her phone. She had paid the deposit for the flowers last week, which she'd budgeted for, but it still took a larger chunk of her last paycheck from Mill City Physical Therapy than she would have liked. She did have a few additional dollars from her share of the tips last night, but Tuesdays were never big money-making nights at Gina's Italian Grill, her side hustle. Too many people were there for the Twofer-Tuesday Special—two giant meatballs for the price of one. Special nights never had enough alcohol sales to bring in large tips. She was scheduled for Saturday this week—that would help. She needed a good night of tips to replenish her bank account and help fund her half of the wedding dress.

Nora's parents didn't have a lot of money, but her mom and dad had agreed to help Nora purchase her dream dress from The Little Wedding Shop. And it really was her dream dress. It was a gorgeous creamy silk and organza ballgown that made her feel like a 1950s Hollywood star. She'd already planned a classic up-do to match the dress's nipped waist and full skirt. She wasn't a very glamorous person in her day-to-day life, but she couldn't wait to try on the dress and feel like. . . well, like a movie star.

Nora hopped in the shower that was jerry-rigged with a metal frame to an old bathtub. The free-standing, clawfoot tub was one of her favorite things about the apartment. It was quaint and, in its own way, glamorous, but from a different era than her wedding dress. Nora quickly scrubbed her scalp and lathered her body. Once she was clean and clothed in her usual jeans, t-shirt, and cardigan, and her hair was blown dry, she unearthed her rarely-used makeup bag. She looked questioningly at some of the cosmetics that were definitely past their prime. *But aren't those expiration dates just one more way the cosmetics industry makes money?* For her skin's sake, she hoped so.

Nora carefully applied the ancient mascara. As she slowly dabbed the lashes at the inside corner of her right eye, her phone chimed. Startled, she jumped and smeared thick black goop across her eyelid. "Dammit, Wanamaker," she swore to herself. She picked up her phone with one hand and grabbed a tissue with the other. Her heart fell a little when she saw the text was not from Brad, but from her mother: **We're looking forward to seeing your dress today, sweetie! Don't forget your wedding shoes.**

"I wasn't going to forget," Nora mumbled as she typed: **Thanks, mom! See you soon!**

Truthfully, she probably would have forgotten, but her mom didn't need to know that. Nora wiped the misplaced mascara, smearing it farther over her face in the process.

She really needed to pick up some makeup remover. Or get some of those face wipes. *But aren't they bad for the environment?* Well, maybe she'd find some compostable ones.

Nora finished her makeup and grabbed her azure, peep-toe wedding heels, shoving them into a Minnesota Public Radio tote bag before heading to the kitchen to start the coffee. As she measured out the grounds, the pile of origami paper on her thrifted kitchen table caught her eye. She really needed to get moving on her crane making for the wedding. She picked up a stack of papers and took them to the tote holding her shoes. She slipped in the squares with care trying not to bend the corners—maybe she'd have some downtime to fold before she had to be back to the office. Nora wasn't all that crafty, but as a middle schooler she'd checked out a library book about origami and fallen in love with the art form. For the wedding, she planned to decorate the tables with cranes and make a backdrop for the ceremony with white paper cranes, silk flowers, and fishing line. Currently, she had about twenty cranes folded. *Only two-hundred-thirty to go!* She had time. The wedding was still six weeks away. The butterflies gathering in her stomach flapped their wings at the thought. *Only six weeks?* She was excited, but she still had so much to do!

As the coffee brewed, Nora stuck her head in the fridge, hoping to find some breakfast inspiration. *Eggs? Too much work. Fruit and yogurt? Are those berries already molding? I just bought them two days ago!* She shut the fridge with a sigh and opened the cupboard, rummaging around until she found a dry, crumbly granola bar. It would do—and even allow her to be honest if her mom asked if she'd had breakfast. With her hand, Nora crunched the wrapper, turning the bar into loose granola. She opened the packaging and poured the crumbs into her mouth, just like she'd done as a kid. The dry, sharp bits of oat came out of the wrapper faster than she expected—Nora coughed, choking on the mouthful of oats, seeds, and nuts. Hacking and spitting the granola into the sink, she leaned on the counter to catch her breath.

Brushing crumbs off her t-shirt, Nora gave up on her half-hearted attempt at breakfast. She grabbed the coffee pot, filled her favorite travel mug, splashed in a little half-and-half, and glanced at the clock on the microwave. *Shit— how did it get so late?* At this rate, she'd have zero time to find street parking and still be on time for the appointment. Snapping up her nearest shoes—a worn-out pair of Adidas sneakers—she pulled them on, grabbed her tote bag, and dashed out the door.

~

"Ugh, move!" Nora moaned at the driver ahead of her, still idling at the intersection after the light had turned green. She looked nervously at the clock on her dashboard: 9:56.

The Little Wedding Shop was just around the corner, but as she feared, the street parking nearby was completely full.

Nora neared Treasure Trove, the thrift store that inexplicably always seemed to have more green clothing than any of the other stores Nora frequented. She wasn't going to complain, though. She liked wearing green—it brought out the green in her hazel eyes. There was no parking in front of Treasure Trove, either. She briefly considered parking in their lot, but nixed the idea, not wanting to take a space since the store supported a charity. Then, she spotted it!—an empty parking lot just down the street. As she turned her Civic toward the open expanse of concrete, she saw the sign: PARKING FOR LUCKY DRAGON CHOW MEIN CAFÉ CUSTOMERS ONLY. ALL VIOLATORS WILL BE TOWED.

She paused the car in the lot entrance and checked the clock again: 9:58, wait, now 9:59. "Screw it," she said and pulled into the first spot. If she didn't get towed, she'd stop into the place for lunch after the appointment. That seemed like the most appropriate way to skirt the rule. Plus, she liked Chinese food—it wasn't like eating it would be any sort of hardship. Nora killed the engine, grabbed her bag, and hurried down the street to The Little Wedding Shop. Forcefully exhaling upward to clear the hair from her face, she entered the shop and was immediately greeted by her mother, Deb and her father, Jim.

"Sweetheart!" Nora's dad said, throwing his arms open wide for a hug. Nora smiled and happily walked into his embrace.

"There you are," Deb chided after Nora and Jim quit hugging. She smoothed the wayward hair on her daughter's head, and said, "I was about to call you."

"It's 10:01," Nora replied in an exasperated tone that said don't start with me. . .

"Well, no matter—let's see this dress!" said her mom, turning back to the saleswoman she'd been chatting with before Nora came in. "We're ready now!"

The saleswoman who looked to be about twenty-five, with perfectly coiffed blond hair and flawless skin, turned to Nora. "My name is Chloe and I'll be helping you today. Would you like anything to drink? Coffee? Mimosa?"

Although a mimosa might have taken the edge off this interaction with her mom, Nora was due back at the office that afternoon. In her rush to be on time, she'd forgotten her travel mug of coffee in the car—she needed the offered caffeine. "Coffee, please. A little cream if you have it?"

"Coming right up!" said the perky Chloe before she disappeared into the room behind the checkout counter.

"Now, how much is this dress, again?" Deb asked, a lifetime of fretting about money dripping from every word.

Nora took a deep breath then spoke with the speed of a pharmaceutical spokesperson reading the fine print. "It was originally $3,000, but they're only charging me $2,400. I'll cover $1,400 of it. All I need from you guys is $1,000, like we talked about a couple of weeks ago when we had dinner together." She hoped her fast delivery would somehow make the amount easier for her mother to hear.

"That's almost double what we agreed on, Nora," Deb said, cocking her head to one side. "Are you sure you can't find a dress that costs less?"

"Debby, it's fine. We can figure it out," Jim said, trying to diffuse the situation.

"I already ordered it and gave them the down payment. It's *my* dress we're seeing today—we're here for *my* fitting," Nora said. She was hoping, without much optimism, that her firm words would end the discussion.

"You know, I'm sure they've had people back out before. People cancel weddings all the time. We could just look at some other options. What about looking at some thrift stores? I know you love those."

"We've been over this, Mom. I don't want a used wedding dress. It just seems like bad luck." Don't only women who get divorced donate their dresses?

"Um, how are we doing?" Chloe said. The store clerk looked noticeably less perky, likely having overheard the end of the tense mother-daughter exchange.

"We're great," Nora said, quickly taking the delicate porcelain coffee cup from Chloe's hand. "Lead the way." Nora and her parents followed Chloe to the dressing rooms at the back of the store. Nora's mom attempted to pause at the rack that read CLEARANCE - FINAL SALE, but Jim grabbed her arm and tugged her along.

Chloe pulled back a curtain, revealing a large dressing room where Nora's dress hung in a place of honor. It was just as beautiful as she'd remembered, with its cascading cream silk and embroidered organza overlay. It was elegant and classic.

"Ohh," her mother made a little sound and put her hand up to her mouth. "Nora, that is breathtaking."

"And you haven't even seen it on her, yet!" Chloe said, cheered slightly by Deb's reaction. Chloe ushered Nora into the fitting room and pulled the curtain. "Put it on as far as you can, then let me know when you need a hand with the buttons."

Nora put down her coffee and slowly undressed, looking at the gown. When she'd picked it out, she hadn't paid attention to the price. *I mean, if you get married to the right person, you only need to do it once, right?* She'd cringed a little at her thoughts, having almost married the wrong man twice before. But this time was different—Brad was Mr. Right. He was perfect, just like the dress. She carefully slipped the delicate silk confection over her head, putting her arms through the off-the-shoulder straps and hugging the bodice to her torso with crossed arms so that the dress didn't fall to the floor. "I'm ready," Nora called to the sales floor.

Chloe opened, then closed, the heavy floral curtain, joining Nora in the dressing room. "This is one of my favorites," she said while fastening the tiny buttons that climbed the back of the dress. "It's just so vintage, you know?"

"Yeah, I think that's why I tried it on," Nora said. "It makes me feel very old Hollywood."

"That's totally it!" Chloe said, slipping the final few buttons through the silky loops. "Okay, ready to show your parents?"

"I'm ready." Hearing Nora's words, Chloe dramatically swept back the fitting room curtain.

Nora's parents, who had settled into the couch beside the large, three-panel mirror, looked at their daughter.

"Wow, sweetheart! You look fantastic!" Jim said.

Nora's mother said nothing, but buried her face in her hands.

"Mom, what's wrong?" Nora hoped she still wasn't fretting about the price tag.

Deb looked up with tears trailing down her face. "I just never thought I'd see this day. My little girl, finally all grown up and getting married." Nora, at thirty-five-years-old, tried not to be offended that her mother didn't see her as a grownup already. She knew her mom meant well— even when she undermined Nora's confidence and made her feel like she was still twelve.

"So, does this mean you like it?" ask Nora, swishing the multiple layers of skirt to and fro before giving the dress a dramatic twirl.

"Honey, it's perfect," Deb said, with the first smile Nora had seen on her mother's face since she'd arrived at the bridal shop.

~

"Well, how was I supposed to say no after I saw you in that dress? You planned that, didn't you?" Deb playfully knocked her shoulder into Nora's as they left The Little Wedding Shop. Nora's father, needing to get back to work, had left shortly after seeing the dress. Nora and Deb had spent the rest of the appointment talking with Chloe about minor alterations and picking out accessories, like a little fascinator-style veil, and debating whether the dress needed a belt. Her mom hadn't even flinched when she'd handed over her credit card at the end of the hour.

Deb couldn't quit talking about the upcoming wedding as she and Nora walked from the wedding shop. She'd been so busy singing Brad's praises, that she'd walked right past her own car. Nora hadn't had the heart to stop her mother—it was so seldom anymore that Deb seemed excited about anything that Nora did. But, as they neared the Lucky Dragon parking lot, Nora slowed her steps and broke through Deb's happy chatter. "I'm going to run in here and grab some lunch before work."

"You didn't pack a lunch?" Deb asked. Nora's mom was firmly in the "we have food at home" camp when it came to eating at restaurants.

"I didn't have time. See you later, Mom," Nora said, not wishing to explain herself further. She kissed her mother on the cheek. "Your car's back that way." She pointed toward her mom's sedan before ducking into the Lucky Dragon Chow Mein Café.

"We're not open ye—" said a man folding a square of paper atop a glass display case full of knickknacks that served as a host stand. He'd paused as he'd looked up and met Nora's eyes. He cleared his throat. "Um, we open at 11:30."

"Oh, I'm so sorry, I'll come back. I just wanted to get some food here to pay you back—I kinda used your parking lot this morning." The confession spilled out of Nora before she could stop it.

The man, who appeared to be in his mid-thirties, pushed back his black hair that clearly needed a trim, and smiled at Nora. "It's okay, people do it all the time. I only call the tow company when they park overnight."

"Oh, that's a relief. . . I guess I'll just have to come back later to repay the kindness," Nora said, turning to the door.

"No—wait—," said the man behind the counter. "I can see if we've got anything ready so you don't need to leave hungry. Do you like egg rolls?"

"I love egg rolls," Nora said, flashing a broad smile that reached all the way to her eyes.

"Coming right up. Take a seat wherever—" The shaggy haired host gestured toward the restaurant's nicked tables and red vinyl booths before walking to the kitchen.

Nora took a seat and looked around. She'd never been inside the Lucky Dragon before, usually getting her Chinese food from China Garden. Despite the somewhat shabby interior, she liked the vibe of the place. It felt somehow familiar to her. Nora looked at the counter where the host had been standing and noticed what he'd been working on when she'd walked in—it was an origami crane. *Huh, what a funny coincidence.*

The kitchen door opened, and the man came out holding a plate with two egg rolls and a cup of sweet-and-sour dipping sauce. He set the plate in front of Nora. "Be careful, they're fresh out of the fryer. Can I get you anything else? Fried rice? Lo mein?"

"Oh, you don't have to do that. This is perfect, really," Nora said.

"My name's D'Wight, if you need anything else." The young man began to turn back to the counter.

"Actually, I was wondering about your origami," Nora said, gesturing to the crane on the counter. "I like folding paper, too. Do you take requests?"

"Funny you should ask that." D'Wight smiled, pushing his hair back again. "I have an Etsy store. I do a lot of special orders—I'm actually trying to finish an order right now. I'm doing this big floating crane backdrop for a wedding and it's taking a lot longer than I thought it would."

"Oh, I'm making a backdrop like that for my wedding too—right now, actually," said Nora, chuckling at the coincidence. "I try to carry paper with me so that I can fold whenever I get a chance. I'm worried I'm going to run out of time before it needs to be done. How long has it taken you so far?"

"Hmm, I'd say I've put maybe fifteen hours into it? I'm only about half done. I need a total of one thousand cranes to complete the job. On the bright side, I think making one thousand cranes means I'll be granted a wish."

"Oh, like *Sadako and the Thousand Paper Cranes*?" said Nora, referencing a book she'd read during her children's literature class in college about a girl with cancer who tried to make a thousand origami cranes so she could wish herself well.

"Yes, exactly! It's an old Japanese legend—maybe a little weird for a Minnesotan of Chinese descent to believe in, but hey, it's worth a shot. I think it's always worth it to believe in a little magic," said D'Wight.

Nora took a bite of a steaming egg roll, immediately spilling shredded cabbage all over her lap. D'Wight chuckled while Nora's cheeks reddened.

"Tell you what, you finish your egg rolls and then I'd be happy to help you fold a few cranes for your backdrop," said D'Wight, handing Nora a napkin.

"Really?" she said, taking the napkin and picking cabbage off her jeans. "But you have so much to do. Plus, I don't have the money to pay you right now."

"These would be on the house," D'Wight smiled and flipped his hair out of his eyes.

~

"How long have you been doing origami?" Nora asked, folding the square of white paper into a triangle. After finishing her egg rolls and going to the restroom to wash her hands, she joined D'Wight up at the host stand with her tote bag of paper.

"Oh, I started when I was a kid. I loved all kinds of art, but found I had a knack for folding paper. I think my parents were a little annoyed that I didn't get into something more Chinese, like calligraphy or paper cutting, but they still supported me through art school. Well, they supported me as long as I was willing to keep running the restaurant, I guess," D'Wight said quickly finishing another crane while he spoke.

"I started as a kid, too. Although, it's just a hobby for me," said Nora, folding the paper into a diamond.

"I find it really meditative. I'd probably still do it, even if people weren't paying me." D'Wight grabbed another piece of paper just as the chime over the front door rang.

Two forty-something men wearing khakis and polos embroidered with company logos walked in.

D'Wight dropped the paper. "Hello! Welcome to the Lucky Dragon. Please take a seat wherever you like and I'll bring out some menus and waters," he said, turning on his hosting smile.

While the two men found a table, D'Wight turned to Nora. "Wow, time flies when you're folding. I'm sorry we have to cut this short—I've enjoyed talking with you…" D'Wight paused, "I just realized I never got your name."

"Oh, I'm Nora."

"Well, it was a pleasure to meet you, Nora," D'Wight said, gathering the cranes that he'd made into a pile and sweeping them into a takeout bag. "Here, it's not much, but you're now a few cranes closer to having your backdrop done."

"This is really kind of you. Can I pay you? For the egg rolls, I mean," said Nora, picking up what remained of her paper and taking the bag from him.

"No need. Just promise you'll come back for a real meal sometime soon. You can pay me then," D'Wight said as he picked up two menus and turned to help his latest customers.

Nora smiled to herself as she tucked the new cranes carefully into her tote bag and headed to the door.

CHAPTER 3 ~ SALLY

Sally drove across town to Treasure Trove Thrift. TTT wasn't as big as Second Chances, but Sally thought their mission was just as important as that of the hospice. TTT supported the work of Children in Need, an organization that helped mothers on the run from abusive relationships. Sally parked her SUV at the back of the store and carried the IKEA bag full of green clothing and linens to the donation door and knocked. When no one answered, she entered the keypad code and let herself in.

"It's Sally," she called toward the front of the store as she unloaded all the green merchandise onto a counter in the narrow messy room where items were sorted and priced. With her bag empty she walked through the back hallway to the front of the store and said hello to Bev who was sitting behind the checkout counter. Sally went about her business filling her bag with yellow and red clothing. By the time she'd finished, other than the racks of blue jeans, almost all the clothing in the store was shades of green or brightly patterned prints. The racks looked like the rows of a flower garden in early summer.

"Good to see you," said Bev as she rang up Sally's purchases. "I was getting nervous—we haven't seen you lately."

"Yeah, I've been busy with grandkids—I don't know if I've ever mentioned it, but my oldest daughter has twins. I love the little rascals, but, they sure can be a handful."

"I bet—I can handle one kid at a time, but two, man, that's gotta be hard."

"It certainly is when they're little. It'll be nice for them when they get older though—having a built-in playmate and all."

"That's true." Bev paused and cleared her throat. "That'll be $32.50."

Sally gave Bev two twenties. As Bev handed her the change, she cleared her throat again. "Um, Sally, why is it that you buy up all of our yellow and red stuff? I know it's none of my business, but I'm really curious."

"It's just my way of donating to causes that I support. I like what Children in Need does for the community. Of course, I'd prefer it if there wasn't a need for their services, but I don't think that's going to be the case anytime soon."

"Wouldn't it just be a lot easier to donate money?" Bev asked.

"Sure, but where would be the fun in that?"

"I guess," said Bev while shaking her head and hefting the refilled IKEA bag toward Sally.

It was a half-truth. Sally did like the work done by Children in Need—serving the women and children in her community. She also believed in the work of the hospice and the local Kitty Cat Shelter. The shelter was the beneficiary of Twice Nice in St. Paul, the third thrift store that Sally supported by purchasing red and green stuff and donating yellow items. But, the real reason that Sally didn't just donate money was her husband, Bruce. Bruce did not believe in charity.

It wasn't that Bruce was cheap. He wasn't, really. He had no problem with Sally spending money on almost anything she wanted. He just didn't want Sally giving their money away. He was, what one of Sally's old friends had called a "bootstrapper"—an individual who thought people (and organizations, evidently) should make it through life without handouts and pull themselves up by their own bootstraps. He'd done it, been born without a silver spoon in his mouth, and he was now the owner of a business that had branches in multiple cities. He thought if he could succeed on his own, anyone with gumption could do the same. Sally thought what Bruce failed to take into consideration was that some people born without tarnishable flatware in their mouths are also born without boots on their feet. Having been through far more adversity, Sally had more empathy than Bruce—what she didn't have was the confidence to question her overly opinionated husband.

Trudy had been the one to give her mom the idea of using thrift store shopping and donating as a way to benefit local charities. When Sally had mentioned to Trudy that she'd purchased a lamp at Treasure Trove Thrift, but then decided it didn't match the colors in the room where she'd intended to use it, and so had donated it to Second Chances, Trudy had said, "Wow Mom, you managed to donate to two organizations in a way that Daddy can't complain about. If you could figure out how to do that on a bigger scale, you could give away a lot more of Grandpa and Grandma's money." And thus it began—Sally's Thrift Store Color Distribution System, or the *TSCDS* as she'd come to think of it.

Originally, Sally had thought she'd work with clothing in the three primary colors, but soon realized that purchasing blue clothing would be nearly impossible given the world's love affair with denim. She settled on red, yellow, and green clothes and then decided that she would purchase anything that was fabric—as long as it wasn't upholstered furniture. Sally was dedicated, but saw no reason to wreck her back being altruistic. It was an expensive proposition at first, buying so much clothing and so many linens. She had worried that Bruce might notice, but when he hadn't, and when she'd realized that after the initial purchases the weekly follow-ups would cost far less, Sally had dedicated herself to the process. She'd been making her TSCDS rounds nearly every week for a year.

Sally checked the clock on her dash. It was a little early for lunch, but her favorite Chinese restaurant was only a block from Treasure Trove and on the route to Twice Nice. Besides, she was hungry.

Sally had first noticed the Lucky Dragon Chow Mein Café when she'd started thrifting shortly after her family had moved to Minneapolis. It had intrigued her because it was housed in a free-standing brick building with a parking lot by its side. So few restaurants in the Twin Cities had parking lots, and so few Chinese restaurants occupied such substantial brick buildings. These days, most chow mein joints were in strip malls or reconfigured Pizza Huts. After her first visit to the Lucky Dragon, Sally was hooked. The restaurant featured a lunchtime special; once she'd tried it, she'd stopped opening the menu. It consisted of a thinly-hammered pork cutlet, breaded and fried, served with a scoop of white rice topped with soy sauce gravy, a cream cheese filled wonton, hot tea, and a fortune cookie—all for only six dollars! Cheap, filling, and tasty was a winning combination in Sally's eyes—and mouth.

Sally pulled into the nearly empty parking lot just in time to see her daughter, Trudy, climbing into a pale blue Honda Civic. She laid on the horn and waved frantically only to feel like a fool seconds later. The woman wasn't Trudy. Why had Sally even thought it could have been her daughter? Sure, they were about the same size and had similar features, but Trudy was at home with the twins. Besides, Trudy drove a burgundy mini van—it was the only vehicle that could handle two car seats, a double stroller, and all the paraphernalia it took to keep two toddlers functioning outside their home environment. Sally quickly looked away and busied herself parking on the opposite side of the lot. Maybe Trudy's doppelgänger hadn't noticed. . .

"Hello, Sally!" said D'Wight as Sally opened the glass front door of the restaurant. D'Wight Wong was the third generation of his family to operate the Lucky Dragon—or so it said on the back of the menu. D'Wight's grandparents had purchased the brick building that housed the restaurant in the early 1950s, and according to D'Wight, the building had an interesting, if somewhat checkered past—not the sort of information his parents would have chosen to include on the back of the menu. D'Wight had told Sally during one of her many lunchtime visits that in the 1920s the upper floor of the two story building had housed a bordello and the basement had been occupied by a speakeasy. The first floor during those years had been a magic shop which it was believed served primarily as a cover for the illegal enterprises going on above and below it. By 1953, the building had been standing empty for over a decade, and D'Wight's family had been able to buy it for far less than they would have had to pay for other properties in the area. It had been a wish come true for the Wongs.

"Hi, D'Wight," Sally said.

"Let me guess—you're here for the special." D'Wight said while shoving the heavy Korean boyband bangs from his eyes. A life-long Minnesotan, he wore a plaid flannel shirt and jeans on his slim six-foot frame and pronounced the letter O like he was auditioning for a role in the remake of *Fargo*. When he was young, people called him cute. As a thirty-six-year-old man, he was handsome in an understated way.

"I feel like I should say 'no' just to mess with you, but you know me too well—I want the special."

"Go on, mess with me. Nothin' could bring me down today." D'Wight said.

"I thought you looked extra cheery—so, you're just that happy to see me?"

"Oh, I'm always happy to see one of our regulars, but the grin's actually for a new customer. I think I just met the girl of my dreams."

"Just met? Do you mean that young woman I saw getting into a car in your parking lot?"

"Yup. She's pretty, seems nice, and can fold a mean origami crane—like I said, the girl of my dreams. Only problem is, seems she's got a fiancé—but I don't give up easily," D'Wight said as he stroked the red ears of the lucky cat waving at Sally from beside the cash register.

"Did you get her name? She looked kinda familiar to me."

"I got a first name—Nora. She's promised to stop in again, so I plan on knowing her last name and phone number within a week or two." D'Wight paused, picked up a small folded crane, smiled at nothing in particular, then returned his gaze to Sally. "So, your regular table and the special, per usual?"

"Almost, but with one little change. Could you have the kitchen split it and put part in a takeout container? My husband's out of town again, and my daughter's eating with a friend, so I'm going to have half of it for supper—hope that's not against the rules."

"It's fine, Sally—I won't tell the lunch special police. I'll even throw in a second fortune cookie."

"You're a good guy, D'Wight." Sally flashed D'Wight a big grin.

"Shhh. Don't say that too loud—it'll ruin my tough guy persona."

"You have a tough guy persona?" Sally chuckled.

"You would not believe how daily origami bulks up a person," D'Wight said. He scowled, attempting to look like a thug, shook his head to flip his hair out of his eyes and flexed an unimpressive bicep, before escorting Sally to a table by the window and walking to the kitchen to place her order.

~

Trudy rang the doorbell of her parents' house with her elbow. In some ways it was easier to take the boys on outings now that they could stand and walk on their own, in other ways it was not. "Hey, Mom, can you grab Ricco before he dislocates my shoulder?"

Sally crouched down and reached out to the toddler. Ricco let go of his mother's arm and ran into his grandma with such force that he nearly knocked her over. Sally hugged the rambunctious eighteen-month-old as he squealed with delight. Rosco, not to be outdone by his twin, broke loose from Trudy's hand and roared toward Sally and his brother, knocking them both backward and landing on top. All three lay sprawled on the foyer floor in fits of giggles while Trudy stepped through the front door, closing it behind her. Sally pulled herself to a sitting position and helped Ricco with his coat while Trudy disrobed Rosco. The boys freed from their jackets toddle-trotted to the toy box in the corner of the living room. After Trudy helped Sally get up from the foyer floor, the two women headed to the kitchen.

"So what prompted this visit? Not that I'm not happy to see you—I'm always happy to see you—but I know it isn't easy going out with the boys."

"Big news—happy news for us, but I'm not sure that you're going to feel the same way."

Sally put a pumpkin-spice teabag in a mug for Trudy and an English Breakfast bag in a mug for herself. While pouring boiling water from her electric tea kettle she asked, "So tell me—what is it that I'm not going to like?"

"Enrique's been invited to do his residency at Johns Hopkins—it's in Baltimore."

"I know where Johns Hopkins is—what happened with going to Rochester? I thought he wanted Mayo?"

"He would have been fine with Mayo, but Johns Hopkins is—has always been—his first choice. It's his dream, Mom." Trudy avoided her mom's eyes and played with her tea, dunking and re-dunking the fragrant teabag in the golden-brown liquid.

"Well, if that's the case, I guess you've gotta go. . . but you're right, I'm not happy about you guys being so far away. I'm going to miss you so much," Sally said while she, too, worked overtime to keep her emotions in check.

"We'll miss you guys, too. Especially you, Mom, but you don't have to tell Daddy I said that."

"Don't worry—I'll let him know you're moving, but I'll leave out that tidbit. I suppose we'd better go see what the little monsters are doing before they. . ." Sally's words trailed off as she attempted to hide her tears from Trudy.

Trudy and Sally took their tea to the living room where the twins were busy playing tug-of-war with a blue plastic truck. The mother and daughter, so alike, sat on the couch and drank their tea without speaking. It was comforting for both to just be in the same room—something Sally knew that they would miss. Eventually Sally said, "So, how soon will you be going?"

"Right after Thanksgiving. We've rented an apartment in Owings Mills; it's a Baltimore suburb. We take possession December first."

"So soon," Sally said, in a tone that combined both surprise and disappointment.

"I know, Mom, but Enrique's job starts the week before Christmas and it'll take both of us to get moved in and get the boys settled. You understand?"

"Of course I do. . . and I'm happy for Enrique. . . he's worked so hard for this, but. . ."

"I know, Mom. But you and Daddy will come visit—it won't be forever."

"Not forever, but the boys are growing—changing—it'll never be the same, and who's to say your family won't move further away in the future." Sally shook her head, "Oh, don't listen to me—I'm just being selfish. Of course you have to go. . ." Tea forgotten on the coffee table, Sally and Trudy hugged with such intensity that both were having problems breathing by the time they released one another.

~

Tick, tick, tick, ding.

Sally removed the sizzling cream cheese-filled wonton from the toaster oven with a pair of kitchen tongs and dropped it on the plate with the rest of her microwaved leftovers. D'Wight hadn't just included an extra fortune cookie, he'd also slipped a second wonton appetizer into Sally's take-out bag. *That D'Wight's a sweetie, even if he is sabotaging my diet plans,* she thought. *I suppose I could just throw it away, but that would be wasteful.* She'd grown up with her father's dinner table admonition, "There are children starving in Africa." Like all American kids reared in the seventies, she'd wondered how eating her dinner could possibly help African children. But, also like a typical kid of that era, she knew enough to not question her parents' authority; it was her job to please them. *My how things have changed,* thought Sally as she remembered Tiffany's attitude that morning, and even Trudy's announcement just hours earlier.

Maybe that was unfair. Unlike Tiffany, Trudy hadn't meant to be hurtful with the news that she and Enrique were resettling her grandsons halfway across the country. Sally was willing to follow the young family to Baltimore, but with Bruce so invested in his newest company— especially the Duluth project—there was no way he'd be willing to move to the East Coast. Though their initial move to Minneapolis had been Bruce's idea, with the almost exponential growth of his company, Sally was sure he wouldn't move again so soon—or so far. Even with as hard as he'd been working—all the late nights and weekend business trips—she'd never seen him happier.

Sally typed Baltimore into Google Maps: 1,115 miles, or 18 hours and 21 minutes; Sally didn't know which numbers sounded worse. She would be so far away from Rosco and Ricco and their sweet baby snuggles. They were the only humans who made Sally feel good about carrying a few extra pounds. They seemed to appreciate the softness of Sally's body as they snuggled into her puffy breasts and pillow-like mid-section. She thought about the boys' greetings that afternoon when they'd all ended up laughing on the floor. Oh, how she would miss the unconditional love of her grandsons. Maybe she could find some airline that had inexpensive and frequent tickets from Minneapolis to Baltimore, that vacation Mecca of the East. *Unlikely, but maybe?*

Sally scraped a few remnants of rice into the trash and put her dirty plate and fork in the dishwasher. As she closed the dishwasher door with an exaggerated slam, her tears started in earnest. She wouldn't miss only the babies, she'd miss her baby, too. She and Trudy had always gotten along extremely well for a mother and daughter—maybe it had to do with being so close in age. Having given birth to Trudy when she was only seventeen, Sally and Trudy had grown up together. Even more so than most teenage moms and their children, since Sally'd had to relearn everything after the accident. It was as though they'd been twins those first few years. Sally pulled a folded tissue from her jeans pocket, dried her eyes, and walked to the cabinet beside the fireplace in the adjoining family room. She slid a battered photo album from the middle shelf and flipped open the cover. In her mother's flowing cursive, she read: *The Early Years.*

The Early Years, that's the way her mother had thought of those times. As though nothing had come before them and everything to come later would be a storybook "happily ever after." Well, it wasn't true. A lot had happened leading up to those years. Sally had forgotten how to walk and speak after her head had bounced off the windshield, but her memories had stayed intact. She remembered it all, even if her parents had always wished she wouldn't.

~

He went by Ben, but his name was Bentley B. Bradley, III. Sally had thought it made him sound like a character out of a romance novel. To her, he was her sweet *bent brad,* her *crooked nail,* but she'd never told him that. He wouldn't have liked it. He was a serious young man, and he carried his family name with a particular solemnity, perhaps because his father and grandfather had both been district court judges and because both were dead by the time Ben had turned twelve.

Sally certainly hadn't meant to get pregnant at seventeen. It wasn't in her life plan, nor had fatherhood in his early twenties been something Ben had dreamt of, but when the drugstore pregnancy test came back positive, to his credit and true to his nature, Ben had stayed by her side. The night of the accident they had been leaving town, driving to Colorado where they'd heard they could marry without a prolonged waiting period. The baby was due within the month. They felt they had little time to spare.

Sally's parents, having pulled Sally from school before she had started to show, were intent that she give the baby up for adoption—something that neither Sally nor Ben wanted. Sally figured if they were married, no one could take their child away from them. She wanted the baby because it was Ben's. Ben loved Sally, but he'd wanted the baby because he wanted a family. He'd lived alone with his mother for ten years; he'd told Sally that one lonely decade was enough for a lifetime.

Sally remembered being on Highway 81 heading toward Norfolk, Nebraska, when she saw the headlights of the oncoming semi. That was the last thing she remembered before waking in the hospital in Sioux Falls two months later after having been placed in a medically induced coma to give her brain a chance to heal. Ben was dead, but her baby—a girl that her parents were calling by Sally's given name, Sara, was alive and thriving. Her parents, convinced by Sally's injuries that she was going to die, had decided to keep her baby as a replacement daughter. It was a hard concept for most people to accept, including Sally, but the recycling of her name had made her parents' intentions all too obvious.

It had taken nearly two years of hard work for Sally to relearn how to walk and talk. She and Sara, whom Sally had insisted be renamed Trudy, had learned those basics together. When she'd first come out of the coma, Sally had mourned Ben. But, after weeks of hellish grief, she'd committed herself to not dwelling in the past. As much as she missed Ben, she knew that she had to get better for Trudy. She told herself that it was what Ben would have wanted, and she attempted to channel his sober determination as she threw herself into the hours of grueling physical therapy it took to regain basic life skills.

Sally eventually earned a GED and an associate degree in office administration with an emphasis in accounting. That's how she'd met Bruce Munson when she was twenty-three—he was her boss at the liquor distribution company where she'd landed her first clerical job. Seven years older than Sally, Bruce seemed worldly and sophisticated. He was handsome and charming, and when he'd told Sally that he wanted to take care of her and Trudy, in her desire to get on with her life and away from her parents, she hadn't required much convincing.

~

Sally flipped through the photo album, not dwelling on the shots of herself in bed with tubes protruding from all visible orifices, her right shoulder and leg immobilized. Instead, she looked at the pictures of sweet, tiny Trudy in the hospital incubator. Her perfect daughter. Oh, how she would miss her.

Sally un-crumpled the Kleenex from her pocket, wiped her eyes, and blew her nose. Holding the now overly wet tissue by the corner, she walked it to the kitchen trash can and dropped it atop the rice-littered takeout container from the Lucky Dragon. She smiled at the silly logo of a cigar-smoking dragon rolling dice and thought of the life she'd built since moving to Minneapolis. She'd found a few friendly neighbors to get coffee with, and her weekly thrift store work had given her life some purpose. In truth, her life was as it should be: her oldest daughter was excited about heading off with her husband who had just been offered the residency of his dreams; her grandsons were healthy and had loving parents to care for them; her younger daughter was bright, athletic, and ambitious—much like her father. She would go far in this world—but not too soon. Tiffany, Sally reasoned, was only fifteen. She would be by Sally's side for a few more years. Sally patted her stomach. No, things weren't perfect, but life was good.

Thinking of Tiffany, Sally hoped she'd be home soon. Tiffany had skipped visiting with Trudy and the twins, but she'd promised to be home by eight-thirty. It was now eight-twenty. She was rarely on time anymore, but she usually had a good excuse. Or, at least, an excuse. Sally was pondering how late her youngest would be and what her excuse would be tonight, just as Tiffany walked in the kitchen door five minutes early.

"Hi, Moms. How was your evening?" Tiffany said as she hung her coat in the mudroom.

Sally, surprised by the unusual trifecta of timeliness, pleasant greeting, and proper coat placement, did a double take before responding. "Alright, but your sister had some news that's making me a bit sad. It's nothing bad, it's just— "

"Just that she's moving to Baltimore?"

"Yeah, how did you know?"

"She told me that it was looking good for Enrique when I saw her last week—she didn't want to tell you until she knew for sure. She didn't think the news would make you happy, but she and Enrique were really pumped."

"Well, yeah, I understand that, but I'm going to miss them. Baltimore is so far away."

"You'll go visit. It'll be okay, and it's really a great opportunity for Enrique. I mean it's Johns Hopkins—it's his dream residency."

"I know—I'm just being selfish, but I'll really miss the boys. They change so much every month when they're little."

Tiffany walked over and hugged Sally. Sally returned the hug and stepped back. "Wow, you haven't done that in a while—is everything okay?"

"Great, Mom. Just thought you could use a hug."

"You're right—thanks—it was nice."

"K—I'm gonna clean my room before bed. Is there anything you need me to do before I go up? Vacuum? Laundry? Anything?" Tiffany glanced around the room.

Sally stood for a moment in stunned silence. "Are you sure you're my daughter?"

"Can't a girl be nice to her mom? I mean, I can take back the offers—even the hug, if you don't want it."

"No, don't you dare—come give me another."

The two embraced. As Tiffany stepped away from Sally's arms, she asked, "When's Daddy coming home?"

"Tomorrow—around noon if his plans don't change again."

"K—goodnight!" Tiffany called as she bounded up the stairs to her messy bedroom while a bewildered Sally stood with her mouth agape.

Who's stolen my daughter and replaced her with this pleasant avatar?

CHAPTER 4 ~ NORA

"Ouch!" Blood immediately welled on Nora's fingertip. She shook out the hand with the offending digit and grabbed a tissue with the other. Working in a medical office meant a lot of paperwork; it also meant dry skin and scads of paper cuts.

Barb, the office manager at Mill City Physical Therapy, came over from where she'd been filing, opened the drawer next to Nora and handed her a bandage from a box that looked like it had been around since the Bush administration—the first one—which was odd considering they were in a medical office.

"You need to put on more lotion," Barb chided. "It's that dry skin of yours—makes you more susceptible to paper cuts." Barb was always after Nora to moisturize. Nora unwrapped the ratty bandage, blotted the blood on her finger and covered the little cut, choosing to ignore Barb's admonishment. With all her frenetic crane-making lately, she'd already made a mess of her hands.

"You don't want to have bandaged hands in your wedding photos." Barb continued, "You need perfect hands to go with that movie star dress of yours!"

"Maybe I'll wear gloves—they'd be the right style for the dress." Nora shrugged and stapled together the papers she'd been working on before her injury. She looked them over twice to make sure she hadn't dripped blood on any of them.

It had been a week since Nora had tried on her wedding dress and shared the photos with Barb, who now talked about the dress and wedding incessantly. It had also been a week since she'd visited the Lucky Dragon and met D'Wight. Talking and folding with him had been nice. She wondered if he could use an assistant with his Etsy orders. Her side hustle could use a side hustle right now with all the wedding expenses. D'Wight had refused to let her pay for the egg rolls if she promised to come back for more food sometime. Maybe she'd grab lunch there today and see if he was around. . . just to pay him back and ask if he could use her help with folding.

Dr. Rogers came out of the exam room, followed by a patient. "Now, take care of that shoulder like I taught you, okay? Have a great day, Ronda," he said, waving at the patient as she pushed open the office door. "And how's everyone doing out here?"

"Doing well," Nora said brightly. "Actually, Dr. Rogers, I've been meaning to ask if we could talk." After looking at her student loan balance a few nights earlier, she'd decided it was time to work up the courage to ask for a raise. She'd been at the clinic since moving back to Minneapolis following her failed relationship with David five years prior and, in all that time, she'd been receiving the same salary.

"Of course. I have time before my next patient." Dr. Rogers leaned on the counter, looking like a doctor right out of *Grey's Anatomy* with his white coat and boyish good looks. His lopsided smile and easy charm were the reason most patients at Mill City Physical Therapy were older women.

"So, as you know, I've been working here for almost five years—" said Nora, looking anywhere but in his intense blue eyes.

"And I don't know what we'd do without you," Dr. Rogers interrupted, flashing his famous grin.

"Um, thank you. So, for that reason, I was wondering if we could talk about my compensation." Nora's voice went up about two octaves at the end of the sentence.

"Oh," said the doctor, his grin falling as he looked at his watch. "Um, I just remembered something I need to get done before my next patient. How about we discuss this another time?" Dr. Rogers looked away from Nora and addressed Barb, "Send Jane Jorgensen back as soon as she gets here." He scooped up a file and disappeared back into the exam area.

"Oh. . . okay, no problem," Nora said to Dr. Roger's back, trying to sound cheery despite the deflection.

Barb shook her head. "You've got to stand up for yourself, girl. Make him listen to you," she said, slamming shut the file drawer. "Otherwise, he's going to treat you exactly the way that you let him."

Nora stood up, "I'm going to get lunch," she said a bit too brightly, not acknowledging Barb's comment—it wasn't as if she'd said anything to come to Nora's defense. "I'm getting Chinese. Do you want anything?"

Nora pulled into the last parking spot in the Lucky Dragon lot. It wasn't the closest Chinese place to her office, but she needed the drive to blow off steam, both from Dr. Roger's avoidance and Barb's comments. Barb didn't know what she was talking about. Nora stood up for herself. She'd brought up the raise, hadn't she? It wasn't like she was mistreated at work. Things were fine. She just thought she should get paid a little more, that's all. Barb was too pushy anyway.

Nora was still brooding when she entered the restaurant, almost missing the sign on the door.

LUCKY DRAGON CHOW MEIN
CAFÉ CLOSING 9/30

GOING OUT OF BUSINESS
RUMMAGE SALE 10/6

"Oh no," Nora said aloud to the sign. She had only just met D'Wight, but already felt like he was a friend after they'd folded cranes together.

Nora walked in to find the restaurant packed with people. It seemed strange that such a popular spot would be shutting down, but maybe word of the restaurant's closing was spreading, and the café regulars were coming in for one last helping of their favorites. D'Wight was with a customer at the checkout counter but looked up when Nora entered. He gave her a big grin and a wave.

Nora waited until D'Wight seated the party waiting in front of her and approached the counter as he returned.

"You came back!" D'Wight said. He'd gotten a haircut since Nora had last seen him, but still cocked his head as though he were flipping hair from his smiling eyes.

"I did," Nora said and smiled back before she remembered the sign on the door. "But I'm sorry to see that your restaurant is closing."

"Well, yeah, but it's a good thing. I got an amazing offer to sell the building out of the blue," D'Wight said. "It was more money than I ever imagined this old place was worth. Plus, the lawyer who brokered the deal said the buyer will let me keep living in the apartment upstairs—rent free!"

He pointed up, indicating that he lived on the second level of the two-story building.

"Wow, that really is amazing."

"I know! Running this place was never my dream. I inherited it from my parents—sort of. My sisters didn't want anything to do with it, so I bought them out. Anyway, with the money from the sale, I'll be able to open my own art studio. I'm looking at a loft in the Northeast Arts District."

"Oh, that's great. I'll miss your egg rolls, though," Nora said.

"Right, I suppose you came here for lunch. Do you want a table?" D'Wight said, picking up a menu.

"I actually need takeout if that's okay. I promised my coworker I'd bring her some moo shu pork and I'll take my regular."

"One order of moo shu pork and a double order of egg rolls, coming right up!" D'Wight said with a conspiratorial wink before he turned and walked toward the kitchen.

Nora wasn't the only one who noticed the wink. A middle-aged woman had pushed open the door at the precise moment of D'Wight's departure. Nora felt her neck warm a little and brought her hand up to her throat. *Am I blushing? Because of a wink? No, that's silly.* To distract herself, she turned to the woman who had just entered and said, "The host will be right back, he just went to the kitchen to place my takeout order."

"Looks like you know D'Wight," said the woman as she settled into a chair by the host stand.

"I guess you could say that we're friends, but we haven't known each other long," Nora said, sinking into the worn vinyl chair next to her. "How about you?"

"Just from coming in for lunch over the past year—D'Wight's a friendly guy. . . but, did you see the sign? I can't believe he's closing the restaurant. I was here just last week and he didn't say a word about it."

"Me, too. I guess it was very sudden. Someone gave him a great offer for the building," Nora said.

"You know, I think I saw you last week. I wouldn't normally remember seeing a person I don't know, but you look a lot like one of my daughters—so much so that I thought you were her. I honked. You must have thought I was an idiot."

"I didn't notice. There's so much honking in the city. Anyway, I'd just been in for my wedding dress fitting down the street—I guess I was thinking of other things."

D'Wight returned to find the two women in conversation. "So, two of my favorite customers know one another?"

"Not really," responded Nora. She reached out her hand toward the older woman, "My name is Nora."

"I'm Sally," responded the older woman as she clasped Nora's hand in both of hers.

Looking toward D'Wight, Nora said, "We know each other now—but with the restaurant closing, we'll probably never see each other again."

"Don't say that," said D'Wight. "You both have to come to my rummage sale on the sixth. It's gonna be like a flea market crossed with a gallery opening for my art. There'll be lots of food. Think of it as a party to celebrate new beginnings. You both have to promise to come."

"Count me in," Sally said.

"I'll try," countered Nora.

Later that night, Nora sat on the couch in Brad's Downtown Minneapolis condo, watching a soccer match. She didn't mind soccer, at least it was better than football. Fewer commercials. She scolded herself for not bringing paper to work on her crane folding, but she hadn't wanted Brad to think she'd be bored by the game.

Some people thought it was strange that Brad and Nora were waiting until after their wedding to move in together. For most couples their age, it was a foregone conclusion that they would move in together before even thinking about marriage. And they had talked about it—moving in together—but Nora knew her mother would have absolutely had a meltdown over it. Despite not being all that religious, Deb was a traditionalist and felt very strongly that things in life had to go in a specific order: marriage, cohabitating, children. No ifs, ands, or buts about it. So, to keep the peace, Nora's belongings remained in her Uptown studio though she spent at least three nights a week at Brad's condo.

Brad came out of the kitchen, holding two beer bottles and handed one to Nora as he sat down on the couch next to her. It was an IPA. Nora hated IPAs. Brad usually kept some lighter beers around for her, but she must have drunk them all. Well, once she officially lived here, she could keep the place stocked with the beer she liked.

"Thanks," she said and took a sip, trying not to shudder at the bitter hoppy-ness of the beer. "So, are you busy Saturday? It's Melanie's daughter's first birthday party— remember I told you about it a few weeks ago? I was hoping you could come with me."

"Gee, I would, but you know Saturdays are my long run days," Brad said, taking a swig of beer.

"The party's in the afternoon. I thought if you ran in the morning you'd be able to make it. Melanie asked me if the time would work for you and I told her yes."

"Well, I'm going to be really tired—it's a twenty-mile day—I just don't think I'll be up for socializing," he said, never moving his eyes from the TV.

"Oh, okay. I understand," Nora said. She took a sip from the sweating bottle and almost choked, already having forgotten it was an IPA. She swallowed hard and continued, "So, have you confirmed our wedding date with the DJ yet?" Nora had been doing almost all the wedding planning, but Brad had a friend who DJed weddings on the side, so he'd taken responsibility for the reception music.

"Uh, no, but I'm not worried about it. He'll be there," he said, still watching the screen where the team in red, *New York, maybe*—Nora couldn't remember—was taking a free kick.

"Okay, if you're sure, I won't worry about it," Nora lied.

"Hi Bunny!" Melanie cried as Nora came in her front door, calling her by the nickname that they'd decided on during their freshman year of college. Neither of them could remember why they had chosen animal nicknames for one another, but they'd stuck. Melanie had been Nora's roommate all four years of undergrad. They'd been inseparable, taking the same courses, eating together in the dining hall, and even going on the same study abroad trip to England—one that Nora was still paying off.

"God, it's good to see you," said Melanie embracing Nora.

"Hi Kitty, congratulations on a year of being a mom." Nora gave Melanie an extra squeeze before letting her go. "I know you didn't want gifts for Juliet, but I got you a little something." She handed Melanie a gift bag that held a delicate silver necklace featuring her daughter's birthstone, a sapphire. The gift had been expensive, but Nora had felt guilty for how little she'd seen her friend now that Melanie was a mom.

"Oh, you are so sweet. I'll open it later," she said, placing the gift on the table in the entryway by a growing stack of cards and gift bags. "Where's Brad?"

"He can't make it. New York Marathon training, you know. The race is coming up at the beginning of November."

"That's right after the wedding, isn't it? Are you guys not going on a honeymoon? . . . God, I'm sorry, I should know that. Some matron of honor I am!" Melanie had been a bit MIA during the planning process, but Nora also hadn't bothered to loop her in on much. She'd had her hands full with Juliet, or so Nora had imagined. She didn't want to be an extra burden on her friend, especially since this wasn't the first wedding Melanie had helped Nora plan. She'd been instrumental six years ago in finding a venue and caterer for the Minneapolis wedding Nora had tried to plan from over a thousand miles away. Of course, that wedding to David never happened, but in a way, that had only given Melanie more duties with needing to make all the cancelations.

"We're waiting for a honeymoon. Originally, I was going to go to New York with him, but Brad said, with the race and all the wedding planning, it would be too much to organize one more thing. We're going to do something later—but could you not tell my mom? She still thinks we'll both be leaving for New York right after the ceremony. You know how old-fashioned she is." Nora didn't agree with Brad about not going with him, but she hadn't wanted to start a fight. Besides, she posited, it would be more fun to get away to some place warm at the beginning of next year when it was sure to be cold and snowy in Minnesota.

Melanie opened her mouth as though she were going to say something, but then looked to the door behind Nora as it swung open.

"Mel!" A statuesque blond in a yellow sundress with a beautiful baby on her hip floated into the entryway past Nora and air kissed both of Melanie's cheeks. "Violet is so excited to celebrate Juliet's big day!" A gorgeous, equally tall man holding a diaper bag and beautifully wrapped gift followed the woman inside. Nora recognized the pair from Melanie's Instagram posts and a brief encounter a few months ago when she'd watched Juliet so Melanie and her husband, Mark, could go out for the evening with this perfect-looking couple.

"So good to see you! Mark and I enjoyed that wine you gave us the other night. It was delicious," Melanie said as she accepted the big gift box from the man. "Oh, Darcy and James, this is Nora." She gestured with her free hand to Nora who had shrunk back against the wall.

"Oh, didn't we meet once? Aren't you Juliet's babysitter?" said the blond, Darcy, with a smile that didn't meet her eyes.

"Nora is my best friend from college. She's been a saint—really helping me out with Juliet," Melanie said.

"That's sooo nice. Do you have any kids of your own?" Darcy crooned.

"No, not yet." Nora gave an equally fake smile to Darcy.

"Nora's getting married in a few weeks," Melanie said quickly.

"Oh, congratulations! Is your fiancé here? I'd love to meet him," Darcy said while looking past Nora into the kitchen where most of the party had already congregated. "James is always looking for more people to golf with."

"He couldn't make it. He's training for the New York Marathon," Nora said, feeling her shoulders tense.

"A runner! Do you run as well?" Darcy asked.

Nora, who had never been athletic, opened her mouth to reply. Before she could speak, Melanie chimed in, "Nora's more of an academic. She was always at the top of our class in college. She went to grad school for library science at the best program in the country."

Nora appreciated Melanie's bragging, but internally cringed at the mention of her time at the University of Illinois. She hadn't finished her masters, taking a leave of absence with two semesters left. She'd been dating David at the time; he'd been a year ahead of her in the program and had received an offer with the New York Public Library system to begin upon his graduation. Instead of trying to maintain the romance long distance, David had proposed to Nora and asked her to move to New York

City with him. The engagement had lasted only six months after the move—David met a woman at his new job and asked for the ring back. Instead of re-enrolling in her grad program, Nora had gone home to Minnesota to lick her wounds. She'd planned to go back to Illinois to finish her degree but had gotten comfortable at home. Then she'd met Brad and school no longer seemed like a priority.

"Oh, are you a librarian? Violet loves story time, don't you, Violet?" Darcy nuzzled her daughter's cheek.

"Nora's a non-practicing librarian," Melanie chimed in again, using a phrase that she and Nora had coined after Nora's move back to Minneapolis. "Though, if you ever need a book recommendation, she's a great source! Nobody knows books like Nora."

"I'll keep that in mind." Darcy flashed another disingenuous smile in Nora's direction.

"Order up on thirteen!" the chef, George, called from the kitchen.

Following an awkward afternoon at Juliet's first birthday party surrounded by Melanie's new mom friends, Nora took off for her dinner shift at Gina's Italian Grill—a moderately priced restaurant that had been serving up overly large meatballs to Twin Cities residents for over fifty years.

Nora grabbed the plates from the kitchen pass-through window and delivered them out to an older couple, John and Dorothy, who were Saturday night regulars. "Here you go! One order of chicken parmesan and spaghetti and meatballs with extra sauce. Can I get you two anything else?" Nora said, setting down their usual orders.

"Oh no, dear, this is perfect," Dorothy said. "I just wish you could sit down and tell us all about your wedding plans. The big day has got to be coming up soon."

"Yup, just a little over a month away," Nora said.

"Are you excited?" John asked, already digging into a meatball.

"Oh sure—there's just a lot to do before then." Nora discreetly peeked back toward the kitchen to make certain she didn't have any orders waiting.

"It's really about the marriage, anyway. I'm sure you're excited about the prospect of being married to that good-looking guy of yours?" Dorothy said. Dorothy hadn't met Brad, but Nora had shown her photos of her six-foot-tall, blond, Scandinavian-looking fiancé on one of the older couple's past visits to Gina's.

"Oh, yes. I am," Nora agreed, scoping out the drinks at her next table. She'd need to refill waters soon.

"Well, when you get to be our age, the wedding itself is something you barely remember. It's just one day in a series of great days together," John said and reached across the table to squeeze Dorothy's hand.

Nora's chest tightened a little watching them. When was the last time Brad had held her hand in public? Would they feel like this loving couple in thirty years? Would Brad?

"Excuse me," Nora smiled and hurried back to the kitchen before Dorothy and John could see the tears welling in her eyes.

CHAPTER 5 ~ SALLY

Tiffany called Sally into the kitchen where she had set the counter with the family's best china. She had poured her mother a glass of wine, and from her own wineglass she sipped Diet Coke.

"Fancy table. . . so what's for dinner?" Sally asked as she settled into her spot at the counter.

"Be patient, you'll see when I serve you," Tiffany said. Tiffany pulled a bowl of kale salad from the refrigerator and set it on the counter, then gathered the plates and walked toward the stove to dish up macaroni and cheese. She set a plate on the placemat in front of her mother.

"This looks great," Sally said, spooning kale salad with crunchy tortilla strips onto her plate alongside the pasta. "Where did you learn to make this?"

"Amanda's mom makes these kale things all the time. It's about as hard as making mac and cheese from a box. You just tear open a bunch of plastic bags and follow the directions. I wouldn't have made it if Daddy coulda joined us—I don't think kale's really his thing."

"You're probably right about that, but he's missing out. This looks really good, and you've always done a great job with mac and cheese."

"Thanks—you taught me well: 'Blindly follow the package directions and hope for the best'— I think that's what you said. Tonight, I thought I'd make the salad, too. It kinda balances out the meal. Like, one good for you thing and one not-so-good for you thing," Tiffany replied.

"I don't think that's normally what's meant by a balanced meal, but I like your logic. So, now that we're eating, are you going to tell me why you're doing this? I know it's not my birthday."

"You're right, I do have a request. . . I want. . . I want to move to Spain." Tiffany said, starting slowly, but finishing quickly so that she didn't chicken out.

Sally attempted a swallow. The chopped kale she'd been chewing stopped mid-esophagus. "Pardon?" her question nearly inaudible over her choking cough.

"Not like *forever*, but for part of a year," Tiffany said. "Remember when I told you Amanda was going on that exchange trip—well, she's decided that she can't, and our Spanish teacher asked if I would like to take her spot. It's a really big deal and it'll look really great when I apply for college."

Sally set down her fork and looked at her daughter. "This is a surprise, and I wish your dad was here to weigh in on the decision. It's not one I can make by myself. . ."

"I know, Mom, and I wanted Daddy here, too, but it's like he's never around for supper anymore. I decided I'd ask you first, and maybe you could talk to him for me."

"Well, give me more details. Like, why did Amanda drop out, and why were you selected to take her place? And, just how much will this trip cost? And, where will you be living—city or country? Oh, and when will you be leaving?"

After a long conversation between bites of macaroni and cheese and salad, Sally had to admit that the exchange trip sounded like a good life experience for her daughter, but she told Tiffany she would leave the final decision up to her dad. Sally agreed to tell Bruce that Tiffany wanted to talk with him, but that was all. Tiffany would have to sell her father on the exchange trip on her own. If Bruce said yes, it would be a done deal, and, before the first of the year, Tiffany would be heading to Barcelona.

CHAPTER 6 ~ NORA

Nora hadn't intentionally chosen the day of D'Wight's rummage sale to pick up her wedding dress from The Little Wedding Shop—but she also hadn't not chosen that Saturday. Conveniently, the alterations to the gown had been finished during the week before the open house, and, as a plus, that Saturday worked for her mom. All reasons to visit south Minneapolis that lovely autumn morning.

The trip to the bridal store had been surprisingly painless. Deb had even agreed to pay for the latest alterations once Nora had promised that she would consider the extra amount her parents were kicking in as an interest-free loan. She'd pay her parents back for it. Eventually. Even if it meant keeping her side hustle at

Gina's a little longer than she'd planned. She had hoped, after marrying Brad and combining their finances, that leaving her serving job would make sense. *Oh well, what's a few more months of slinging meatballs three nights a week if it means I get my dream dress?*

Distracted by thoughts of her dress, Nora hadn't noticed the changes down the street at the Lucky Dragon before she'd entered the bridal store, but she certainly noticed them now as she and Deb walked toward the old restaurant's front door. The formerly shabby red brick building was now painted a stunning white. Black shutters and window boxes brimming with lush green plants framed each of the windows. Nora had been surprised that the new owners had worked so fast and even more surprised that they had thought it a good idea to plant live foliage in the fall in Minnesota. *They must not be from around here.*

"Wow, this looks great!" Nora marveled at the revived building as she and her mother walked up to the door bearing a sign reading: RUMMAGE SALE AND ART SHOW TODAY.

"What looks great?" Deb said, not looking up from her phone, which she was holding at waist height, about three feet away from her face.

"You really need to wear your glasses more often, Mom," Nora chided. "This building—don't you remember how it looked before?"

"Huh, I guess I'd never noticed. . ." Deb finally looked away from her phone and squinted up at the facade. "I'll have to take your word that this is better."

"Oh, it's way better! Come on, let's go in." Nora held open the door for her mom and the two women entered the former restaurant. The place was comfortably crowded with people, but Nora quickly spotted D'Wight at the center of a big group of what she assumed were friends and admirers.

"Nora! I'm so glad you came!" D'Wight said, breaking away from his other guests. "Welcome to my art show and rummage sale—the Minneapolis event of the season!" He gestured toward a banquet table of appetizers in steam trays and smaller tables full of kitchen implements and knickknacks for sale. The walls were covered with huge wall hangings featuring thousands of origami cranes. The multi-colored folded cranes were hung so that they created scenes like ocean waves and mountains. D'Wight's pieces put Nora's spindly little crane wedding backdrop to shame.

"D'Wight, these are absolutely amazing! I had no idea you could do something like this with folded paper and string," Nora said. She walked toward a piece near the door to get a better look; it looked like a hurricane made of hundreds of little birds.

"Thank you! I'm really proud of that one," D'Wight said, gesturing to the twisting mass of origami birds. "It's a statement on how something small and seemingly weak on its own—like a bird—can combine with others of its ilk to create something so much stronger and more substantial. Or at least that's what I wrote on the gallery tag."

"Well, that is something," said Deb from behind Nora.

"Oh, D'Wight, this is my mom, Deb. Mom, this is D'Wight."

"It's nice to meet you, D'Wight. My daughter has told me so much about you," Deb said, her smile looking forced.

"Has she really? Well, it's an honor to meet you. I haven't known your daughter long, but I'm already a big fan," D'Wight said.

"I don't know if I've told you all that much, Mom." Nora turned to D'Wight as a splotchy pink blush crept up her neck. "I just let her know that you're the origami artist who helped me fold a few cranes for my wedding backdrop."

D'Wight's face dimmed a little at the wedding reference, but he replied, "Yes, that's me! Happy to help with some more folding if you need it."

"You wouldn't be folding them in here, would you?" Nora's mother sniffed the air of the old restaurant. "I'd hate for Nora's wedding to smell like moo shu pork."

"Um, no. I've just rented an art studio in Northeast Minneapolis. I think most of my folding will be happening there now," D'Wight said, taking Deb's comment in stride.

"Well, we should let you get back to your other guests." Nora gestured to the mix of folks wandering around picking up soup bowls, Chinese tchotchkes, and free egg rolls.

"Okay, but don't leave before saying goodbye! Oh, and here's my new card if you need more cranes for your backdrop." D'Wight handed Nora a business card:

D'Wight Wong, Origami Artist
Studio 206, Casket Arts Building
Northeast Minneapolis
612-555-9876
info@dwongart.net

"Huh, I never would have thought that's how your name was spelled," Nora said, looking up at D'Wight.

"Oh, yeah, I changed the spelling when I was nineteen. I thought it was more interesting—artistic—that way. Now I realize that it just confuses people and makes filling out government forms a pain in the ass." He shrugged.

"Yeah, I can see why," replied Nora. "I'll give you a call if I need more help, which I probably will."

"Sounds great." D'Wight gave Nora a thumbs up and walked away. As soon as he'd struck up a conversation with another group, Nora turned to her mother.

"Mom, I can't believe you asked if the cranes would smell! That's super insensitive, even a little racist."

"It's not racist—it's a Chinese restaurant for goodness sake! Your generation is too sensitive," Deb huffed. "Anyway, I was thinking of you. I thought the smell of

Chinese food at your wedding might remind you of Adam."

Nora groaned at the mention of her undergrad boyfriend and—very briefly—fiancé who ended up breaking off their engagement to backpack across China after college graduation.

"Mom, that was years ago. I've clearly moved on."

"Need I remind you that you wouldn't eat Chinese food for years after he dumped you?"

"I was twenty-two and overly dramatic. And it wasn't years—it was, like, a year."

"Well, you might be thirty-five now, but you're still dramatic," Deb said.

"Gee, thanks, Mom." Nora rolled her eyes.

CHAPTER 7 ~ SALLY

Sally pulled into the parking lot beside the Lucky Dragon, happy to see that it was nearly full. So many cars meant that D'Wight was having a good turnout for his rummage sale-cum-art open house on this first cool Saturday morning of autumn. Sally was sad to see the Lucky Dragon closing, but she would always wish success for a friend embarking on a new endeavor, and, while there was a large gap in their ages, she considered D'Wight Wong a friend. Walking up to the front door she couldn't help but notice the changes being made to the front of the building. The new owners had chosen to paint the brick. *Huh, very unusual color, but I really like it,* Sally thought as she pushed open the restaurant door.

D'Wight had been busy. Everything in the old restaurant had a price tag stuck to it, even the waving kitty statue by the cash register. Sally picked up the golden feline. *Three dollars? What a deal. If it's not sold by the time I leave, I'm buying it,* thought Sally setting the cat back and making her way to the long buffet table full of chafing dishes.

Sally bit into a chubby crab rangoon then immediately regretted her decision. The still-warm cream cheese filling squirted from a corner of the crunchy wonton and slithered down the front of her orange wool peacoat. *Shoot, slimed on its inaugural wear of the season. Shoot, shoot, shoot. . .* And now her fingers were greasy, to boot. Sally picked up a napkin and wiped the white schmutz from her coat before cleaning the top of her shoe and the floor beside it. Heading toward the restroom to wash, she saw Nora standing in front of one of D'Wight's impressive origami wall hangings. Nora was deep in conversation with a brittlely thin, middle-aged woman, but she paused when she noticed Sally.

"Seems D'Wight was right when he said that we'd meet again," Nora said before turning back to her companion. "Mom, this is my new friend, Sally. Sally this is my mother, Deb Wanamaker."

Sally looked down at her hand, wiped it on her jeans, and extended it toward Deb. "Hi, Sally Munson."

Deb took Sally's hand gingerly and acted as though she hadn't noticed Sally's not so clandestine attempt at cleanliness. "I'm happy to meet you. How did you and my daughter get to know one another?"

"Well, I'm not sure we know one another, but we met through this place." Sally's sweeping hand indicated the restaurant. "I guess we were introduced by D'Wight."

"Yes, *D'Wight*. We just met. Nora talks about *him* all the time."

"I do not, Mom. I've mentioned D'Wight a few times—you blow things way out of proportion."

"Well, in my day, engaged women didn't go out of their way to meet new men."

"I didn't go out of my way to meet D'Wight. Can we just change the subject?"

Sally, well acquainted with mother-daughter skirmishes, was happy to help and said, "Isn't D'Wight's work amazing?"

"What he does with paper and string is astounding! I want everything but I've got to wait—wedding bills and all," Nora responded.

"Nora has always liked origami," Deb said.

"Oh, me too, although I don't have the skill to fold anything more complicated than a paper hat."

"Nora's quite good at it. She's been working on a backdrop of folded cranes for her wedding." Sally could sense the motherly pride in Deb's voice. She looked at Deb, studying her features. She could see a mother/daughter resemblance, especially in Nora and her mother's height and hair color, although Sally assumed that, by this point in Deb's life, her shiny brunette locks came from a squeeze bottle.

"Yes, Mom, and that's how I got to know D'Wight." Nora looked at Sally and said, "He's offered to help if I get in a bind—As you can imagine, he's a fast folder."

"A fast folder—I like that," D'Wight said as he walked up behind the three women standing in front of his wall hanging.

"You're much more than that," said Sally. "I had no idea that such wonderful art could be made from origami. I mean, I've seen some pretty spectacular little pieces, but your work makes such big, bold statements. It's kind of like mosaic; little bits of beauty put together to create a finished piece of total splendor—if that makes any sense."

"Yeah, I get it—thanks," said D'Wight. "I'm working on a new website—I might like to use your quote to describe my art, if you don't mind." He handed Sally his business card, "I'd give you credit of course."

When Sally, attempting to be polite, showed the card to Deb, she brushed it aside saying, "Nora already has one. I've seen it."

"I can't wait to visit the new place," Nora said to D'Wight, deflecting Deb's brusque gesture.

"It should be ready next month. I want to have it up and running by Open Casket."

"Goodness, what are you talking about?" asked Deb with an expression on her face somewhere between bemusement and horror.

"That's what they call the big open house at Casket Arts—the building that houses my new studio. It used to be a casket company. The show brings in a lot of people—looking and buying. Or, at least, thinking about buying. The hope is that people will see something and come back to do their Christmas shopping."

"We should all go!" said Nora with enough excitement to make her mother turn and look at her.

"I'd like that," responded Sally. "When is it?"

"November third and fourth. It's always the first weekend in November," D'Wight said.

"Won't you be busy that weekend?" Deb asked, one eyebrow arched toward Nora.

"Oh, darn, you're right. I guess I'll be on my honeymoon."

"Wow, Nora, your excitement is palpable," D'Wight said with a wry grin sneaking across his face.

"No, no, of course I'm excited. But, I mean, it's like your grand opening," Nora responded.

"Yes," Deb said, "and it's *like your honeymoon.*" Deb's darkly penciled eyebrows lifted, making her forehead wrinkles deepen further.

"Deb, are you going to be busy on the fourth? Maybe you and I can plan on attending D'Wight's event and give Nora a report when she returns," Sally said to break the mounting discomfort.

"That would be nice, Sally," Deb said as she turned away from a blushing Nora.

While the two women exchanged numbers, D'Wight, took the opportunity to leave for the kitchen and retrieve a stainless steel chafing dish for the buffet table. Still sensing Nora's angst, Sally tried another diversionary tactic and asked, "What do you think of the new paint color on the building's exterior—kinda bold, huh?"

Seemingly thankful for the change of topic, Nora responded with a puzzled look, "I like it—not sure I'd call it bold, but it really freshens up the place."

Sally fished the shiny statuette from the kitchen trashcan. *How in the world did it get there?* she thought, as she wiped damp coffee grounds from its smooth golden body.

"Tiff, did you throw out my new lucky kitty?"

"No, but looking at it, I can see why someone did. It must have been Daddy—you know how much he hates kitschy crap."

"I suppose, but he really shouldn't have done it. It was a gift from the owner of that Chinese place that I like that's closing."

"Well, if you like the silly thing, you should be able to keep it around. Maybe put it where Dad won't see it?" Tiffany said.

"Where won't he see it? He lives here, too."

"The laundry room—I don't think Daddy ever goes in there."

"Ha, you're right about that." Sally patted the top of the cat's head between its upright red ears, set its arm waving, and carried it from the kitchen.

Bruce entered the kitchen shortly after Sally had walked out. It struck Sally as though he'd been lurking in the hallway waiting for her departure. Sally paused by the laundry room door to listen.

"Hi, Daddy—Mom's pissed off at you for tossing her new pet in the garbage."

"God, that awful thing? There's no way I'm gonna look at that first thing every morning," Bruce said.

"You won't have to. She pulled it out of the trash, but she's putting it in the laundry room."

"Good— Hey kiddo, do you want to ride with me to school today? Your mom told me a few days ago that you have something you want to talk to me about."

"Yeah, thanks. I thought you'd forgotten."

"No, just busy. Go grab your stuff—I want to get outta here before I have to listen to your mom bitching about what I did to her stupid cat thingy."

Sally, still in the laundry room doorway, looked down at the sweet kitty in her hands and shook her head at Bruce's words. She set the statuette in the laundry room but went back to the kitchen when she heard the garage door grinding open. Tiffany nearly out the door, popped her head into the kitchen long enough to say, "Dad's taking me today. See ya."

"Bye, do you—" The door slammed before Sally could finish her question.

Sally was glad that Bruce was driving Tiffany; he usually claimed to be too busy for the extra four minutes it added to his morning commute. *Ahh, maybe Tiff's finally going to talk to him about the study abroad program, or maybe the coward just wanted an excuse to get away before I questioned him about throwing out my cat,* thought Sally. She figured her new statue would be fine in the laundry room, but D'Wight had said that it was supposed to be around people for its magic to work when he'd gifted it to Sally at the rummage sale. Sally had thought when she'd set it on the wide windowsill above the kitchen sink that she'd found the perfect place to give everyone in the house the benefit of the waving kitty's good luck. *Well, it's their loss, not mine. Maybe with it in the laundry room I'll get the rest of the family's share of good fortune.*

Sally hadn't meant for the lucky cat statue to be a gift, but D'Wight wouldn't let her pay for it; he'd insisted she take it as a parting gift from him and the Lucky Dragon. Not that they would never see each other again. Sally was looking forward to visiting D'Wight and seeing his origami creations at his new studio, but it wouldn't be the same, or as frequent, as their almost weekly visits at the restaurant.

The changes already being made at the old Lucky Dragon building had surprised Sally. While the interior hadn't changed except for being rearranged for the rummage sale, the exterior of the building was already undergoing a massive transformation. Gone were all indications that the building had once housed the Lucky Dragon Chow Mein Café. The big windows in the front were covered in brown paper, and the signs were down—even the large neon one of the cigar-smoking dragon rolling dice. The biggest surprise, however, was the new paint color. The old red-brick building was being painted an exotic dusty-lavender. It was one of Sally's favorite colors, but she had to admit that it was an unusual color for the exterior of a brick building, and she'd found it interesting that Nora hadn't been surprised by the choice when she'd mentioned the change at the rummage sale. *Maybe lavender's the new greige. . .*

Sally poured herself another cup of coffee, sat down at the end of the kitchen counter, and stared out the window. Tears puddled in the corners of her eyes as she thought about her conversation with Tiffany earlier in the week. Sally had told Bruce that Tiffany wanted to talk to him, and the discussion was likely transpiring right now, during their commute. Sally had no doubt that Bruce would say yes to Tiffany's opportunity to live in Spain for part of the year. Tiffany was his girl—he rarely said no to her. And, while Sally was pleased for Tiffany, she would miss her terribly, especially with Trudy and the twins leaving too.

Empty nesting was coming sooner than she was prepared for. At least she still had Bruce. He'd always been a bit self-absorbed and overly concerned about appearances, but he'd also been attentive and loving in the early years of their marriage. Maybe with the girls gone they could rekindle some of the spark that had left their relationship. Wasn't that what all the women's magazine headlines said—something like "The Best is Yet to Be?" Perhaps the shiny kitty sitting on the laundry room windowsill would wave some good fortune in Sally's direction, or perhaps it already had by introducing her to Nora and Deb. With all the sudden changes in her life, it was nice to have made some new friends.

Sally wiped her eyes and let out a long sigh. *It'll be all right. . . I'll be all right. . .*

CHAPTER 8 ~ NORA

Nora sat at the bar at Gina's following her Saturday night shift, nursing a Purple Rain. The puckery concoction of vodka, blue curaçao, and grenadine had been created in the 1980s as a salute to Minnesota's royal rocker, Prince. Rumor had it that it was invented by Gina's longtime bartender, Mack. But Mack, being the self-effacing professional that he was, would never admit to its creation. He had, however, introduced Nora to the drink's sweet and tart pleasures, and it had become one of her favorite cocktails. Though, tonight, even the pleasure of a Purple Rain couldn't make Nora smile. It had been a steady night, but the tips hadn't been as good as she'd hoped. She'd need every dollar she could get to pay off her credit card bill full of wedding expenses.

"Why the long face, Peanut?" Mack said as he wiped down the counter, readying to close up for the night. He'd started calling Nora "Peanut" after her first week on the job years ago. She'd begun working at the grill when she was in college and, despite moving away for grad school, there'd been a job waiting for her upon her return. Nora had no idea where the nickname had come from, but she didn't mind it. For some unknown reason, people enjoyed giving her nicknames.

"I guess I'm just worried—I have this nagging feeling that something isn't right. Like something bad is going to happen." She sighed, swirling the melting ice around in the dregs of her now blue-gray drink with a cocktail straw.

"Well, the way I see it, things are gonna happen or they're not gonna happen. Worrying about it is just a waste of time," Mack said before dunking a glass in the bar's dip-sink filled with soapy water.

Nora sighed again. "I suppose that's true. Don't get me wrong, I'm really excited to be marrying Brad, but I have this feeling that I'm just not. . . well, where I'm supposed to be in life. Does that make sense?"

"Peanut, you're exactly where you're supposed to be, and I don't just mean at my bar." The older man gave a knowing smile and a shake of his head. "You're young. You have plenty of time to get wherever it is you think you should be going."

"I'm thirty-five, Mack. I'm not that young."

"Thirty-five's young. Take it from this sixty-five-year-old geezer—you've got time."

Nora glanced at her phone as it lit up with a text from Brad. It was strange to hear from him so late on a Saturday night. He was usually asleep by now, preparing for his early Sunday training run: **We need to talk. Come over to my place tomorrow around 2?**

As Nora stared at the message, a feeling of dread spread slowly throughout her body. Brad had been distant lately. Not responding to her texts, not attending events with her. She'd been dumped by two fiancés before. . . she knew the signs. *No, no, no—I'm just jumping to conclusions. Maybe he just wants to talk about the DJ for the wedding. Maybe his friend can't do it, and we need to come up with a quick plan B. Yeah, that's it.* Nora tried to get her heart rate to slow down as she texted back: **Sure! I'll see you then. Sweet dreams!**

"Everything all right?" Mack asked while he polished a glass.

"I. . . I honestly don't know," Nora said and bit her lower lip. She set down her phone and picked up her glass, the melting ice quaking as she lifted it to her mouth.

CHAPTER 9 ~ SALLY

"But why does it have to be so soon? I thought you said the first of the year," Sally said.

"I don't make the rules, Mom—they want me to arrive at the beginning of December because there's a break in classes. If I go then, I can tour part of Spain with the other exchange students," Tiffany said. "You want me to get the most out of the experience, don't you?"

"Of course I do. It's just that I'm going to miss you and your sister. Neither of you have ever been away at Christmas before. I'm just bummed—can't you let me be bummed for a little while?" Sally said, staring into the refrigerator, her eyes tearing.

"You can be bummed all you want, as long as I can go."

"Yes. . . of course you can go. I'm just being selfish—It'll be a great experience," Sally said with little enthusiasm. She closed the fridge and handed Tiffany the milk carton.

~

Sally drove past the Lucky Dragon during the week's thrift store rounds. The exterior of the building was far more complete this Saturday than it had been the Saturday of the open house. The paint job was nearly finished; the front of the brick building was now completely lavender, and the windows were surrounded by dark green shutters. Window boxes, mounted beneath pristine curtained windows, overflowed with purple and white variegated wisteria. Sally knew that the flowers had to be fake—it was October in Minnesota after all—but they certainly looked real. *Can they be real?* thought Sally. There was still no indication of what the building was to be used for, but Sally assumed it would be only a few days until signs went up. Maybe the building was being transformed into a boutique. . . or a gift store. . . or a tea shop. *It would be so nice to have a tea shop within steps of one of my TSCDS stops. . .*

The idea of a tea shop made Sally think of food; what she wouldn't give for just one more Lucky Dragon lunch special. Maybe she would make something Chinese for supper—fried rice or canned chow mein. She wouldn't have to make much. Bruce was gone again. This weekend he was in Duluth, scouting a location for the newest branch of Munson's Quality Liquors. Sally was happy that the company Bruce had purchased—with the help of her inheritance—had grown so quickly, but she worried that he was overextending himself; he wasn't getting any younger, even if he was dressing as though he were. His new suits were cut to hug his body, and the pants—well, Sally wasn't sure how he sat in them. They couldn't be comfortable, yet Bruce insisted that they were. She was happy that he hadn't decided to dress like his political hero, in those big, boxy suit coats and overly long red ties, but Sally still didn't think it appropriate for a man nearing his sixties to dress like a twenty-something actor either. At least Bruce had the body for it. But, that caused its own problem—because he was slim, Sally was afraid that if she mentioned anything about his suits being tight, he might take it as an excuse to make another cutting remark about her weight. She didn't need that. *Not now*. Although she spent much of her time trying to convince herself otherwise, there was already enough in her life to be unhappy about.

Sally drove down Lake Street, headed toward St. Paul. If she hurried, she could drop off her bag of yellow linens and clothing at Twice Nice and easily beat the afternoon crowd to the grocery store.

~

"Nora! Hey, Nora!" Sally shouted over the rows of used clothing at Twice Nice, "What are the chances we'd meet again so soon?"

Nora walked toward Sally. "Are you sure you aren't stalking me, Sally Munson?"

"Heavens, no. I would be much more subtle if I were. What brings you to downtown St. Paul?"

"Oh, I've always liked this thrift store—I like that it supports the cat shelter. I love cats. Well, dogs, too." Nora pulled a yellow cardigan from the rack in front of her and held it out at arm's length to get a better look.

"We used to have two cats, but the last one died before we left Sioux Falls. Do you have any pets?" Sally asked.

"No—my fiancé is allergic to most animals. Really anything with fur," Nora said with wistful smile as she hung the sweater back on the rack.

"That's a shame. I've always thought of pet ownership as one of the few perks of being a grown-up. You know— as an adult, it's not like you have to beg your parents for a kitty or wish for a puppy from Santa. If you want a cat, or a dog, or, an iguana for that matter, you can just get one."

"As long as your fiancé's not allergic," Nora said, her wistful smile turning more wistful.

Sally'd been tossing items into her cart as she and Nora had continued to talk. Sally could tell that Nora was bemused by her cart of red and green clothing even before Nora said, "Have you ever noticed how much yellow stuff gets donated to this store? It's almost like they request it."

"They don't, but they don't seem to mind, either."

"How do you know?" Nora asked.

"Believe me—I just do. . . speaking of colors, have you seen the Lucky Dragon now that the paint job's done?"

"Yeah, but wasn't it finished last Saturday?"

"No, just part of the front—it's completely lavender now."

"What? You've got to be kidding—it looked so good white. Why would they go and paint it lavender? What kind of color is that for a building?" Nora said, her dismay clearly evident on her face.

"When was it white? Maybe you saw it with just a primer coat," Sally said.

"No—that was no primer." Nora shook her head. "There were even plants in the new window boxes, which I thought strange for this time of year—who does that?"

"Same sort of person who paints a brick building lavender. I think it looks terrific, but I still don't know what sort of business it's going to be. I'm hoping a tea shop." Sally said.

"I've been wishing for a bookstore," countered Nora. "I'd love to see a little indie bookstore go into that space. I'll have to drive by to check out the new paint job. Maybe they'll finally have a sign up." Nora held up a red sweater, and Sally gestured for her to throw it atop the growing pile of red and green clothing in her cart.

"Yeah, and let's hope there's a late frost this year. I'd hate to see those gorgeous purple and white wisteria turn to mush," Sally said.

When Nora continued to look befuddled, Sally changed the subject. "The wedding must be coming up soon—end of the month, right?"

"The twenty-sixth."

"It'll be here before you know it."

"Yeah. . . oh shit." came Nora's panicked response as she glanced at her phone. "Sorry I can't talk longer. I've got an appointment at 2:00. Gotta go."

Running into Nora had slowed Sally's progress and now she was too hungry to go to the grocery store; she knew from past experience that she'd end up buying everything in sight. Perhaps lunch out and a light meal for dinner was in order. She'd always liked the wood fired grill place off 7th Street, and if she drove around Rice Park on the way, she could see the flowers in the seasonally curated front gardens of The St. Paul Hotel. She was sure that the asters and mums would be especially showy this time of year.

Sally slowed to look at the orange and purple blooms that flanked one side of the hotel's crescent driveway. What she saw made her take her foot off the gas and raise a hand to cover her mouth. As he stood under the stately black canopy that led to the gold double doors of The St. Paul Hotel, Bruce slipped his arm around a gorgeous redhead. The woman looked young enough to be his daughter, however, it was clear to anyone with working eyes that she was not. The long kiss he planted squarely on her mouth removed any doubt. The driver in the expensive car behind Sally's Sportage honked his horn. Sally grabbed her steering wheel and stepped on the gas; her SUV spun out with enough force to spray the impatient man's idling Beamer with gravel unearthed from the well-groomed city street.

Sally blew through the stop sign at 4th Street and skipped turning onto 7th. All thoughts of food were gone, exiled from her brain by what she'd just witnessed. She drove home amid the Saturday afternoon stop-and-go traffic with a weight on her chest unlike anything she had felt since her teens—since finding out about Ben. . .

Sally didn't think that Bruce could have noticed her through his friend's curtain of thick hair. Even though he wasn't in Duluth, Bruce wouldn't be home tonight—Sally was certain of that. She'd have time to think about the situation and plan her next moves. . . just as soon as she could remember. . . how. . . to. . . breathe. . .

CHAPTER 10 ~ NORA

After saying goodbye to Sally, Nora left Twice Nice and drove toward Brad's condo in Minneapolis. Maybe it had been a mistake to go thrifting before seeing Brad, but Nora had felt she had to do something to try to get her mind off their afternoon meeting. For sure it had been a mistake to drive all the way to St. Paul with her aging Honda Civic whining whenever Nora took it out on the highway. Hoping to nurse it along a few more months, knowing that she couldn't afford whatever repairs the car might need, Nora opted to take Marshall Avenue through the capital city. Besides, Marshall turned into Lake Street at the Mississippi bridge and would take her past the Lucky Dragon. Nora was curious to see if Sally was right about the building's new color and the wisteria. She couldn't believe that anyone would paint a brick building lavender, but understood the new owners going with fake flowers instead of live ferns after hearing about Minnesota winters.

Seeing Sally had made Nora think about D'Wight. Although, honestly, Nora hadn't needed many excuses to think about the dark-haired paper crane artist lately. She hoped his new studio was treating him well. She had his card. Maybe she could stop in and see him before Christmas. She'd have plenty of time to visit if she wasn't planning a wedding. . . *shit*. . . Nora's stomach dropped as she thought of her quickly approaching "appointment" with Brad. That's what she'd begun to think of their meeting as—an appointment for a truly terrible procedure, like a root canal.

Nora slowed as she approached the former Lucky Dragon building. It looked even better today than it had when she'd seen it a week ago. Maybe the painters had applied another coat of white enamel, because the pristine building seemed to glow. The same very real ferns sprung cheerfully from the window boxes—no purple in sight. *Sally Munson is nuts,* thought Nora as she glanced toward the parking lot beside the building. That's when she noticed him. A shirtless D'Wight stood in sweatpants and stockinged feet with his arms around a petite woman with waist-length black hair. When he released her, she reached up and lovingly rubbed his shivering bare arms before she climbed into a late model MINI.

HONK! Nora hadn't realized she'd slowed to a dead stop, but the driver behind her certainly did. Nora hit the gas, embarrassed that she'd stopped traffic on the busy street with her gawking. She pulled away hoping D'Wight hadn't noticed her. The hug she'd witnessed bothered her more than she wanted to admit. She felt adrift—like she knew nothing, understood no one. Is this what people mean when they talk about their lives spinning out of control? Was she crazy, or was everybody else the problem? As she drove the rest of the way to Brad's, she distracted herself with thoughts of D'Wight and Sally. *Did the woman have dementia? Or just remarkably poor eyesight?* Maybe Sally just saw what she wanted to see—some people were like that. *Am I like that? Did I just imagine D'Wight was interested in me? I mean, not that it matters, but wasn't he? Who was he saying goodbye to? What's wrong with me? What's wrong with Brad? Why don't men stay in love with me. . .*

Nora arrived at Brad's downtown high-rise and parked on the street, paying the $2.50 for an hour of parking. Hopefully it wouldn't take much longer than that for Brad to shatter her dreams. She usually parked in his building's guest spots, but that didn't feel right today—he'd have to come down and sign her in and that sounded more awkward than it was worth. She'd pay the $2.50 to spare at least that much of her dignity.

After she got to the front door and dialed Brad's number on the call box, he buzzed her in without saying anything over the intercom. Nora had to admit that wasn't unusual, but everything today felt like an omen. She took the elevator to the seventh floor; her feet were leaden and her mouth full of cotton as she walked down the long hallway to his door. She knocked, the first time she'd done it in years, but today, after being summoned, it just didn't feel right to walk in.

Brad opened the door. "Nora, thanks for coming—come in," he said much more formally than he normally would have. "Please, sit down." He gestured to the couch.

Nora sat down slowly, clutching her purse on her lap, not daring to set it down in case she needed to make a quick getaway. Brad sat down next to Nora and let out a big sigh. "Thanks for coming," he said again.

"Of course. What's up? Is it the DJ?" Nora said, a last-ditch attempt to assuage her fears.

"The DJ? Oh, no. . . no, it's not that." Brad sighed again. "I've been thinking about it, and, well—I think we should call off the wedding."

"Oh. . ." said Nora. Despite knowing that this was likely the reason she had been invited to the condo, hearing the words aloud still felt like a punch in the gut. "Um. . . why?"

"I was hoping you wouldn't ask that," Brad said, putting his head in his hands.

Nora felt a rare flare of anger and stood up, her purse falling to the floor. Facing Brad, who was still holding his face, she said, "Of course I'm going to ask that! We're supposed to get married in less than two weeks, you idiot!

Why would you call it off? What happened? What did I do?"

Nora's anger had startled Brad out of his stupor. He looked up from his hands, eyes wide. "You—you didn't do anything. It's me. I. . . well, this is hard to say."

"Say. It." Nora said, her teeth clenched, hands balled into fists.

"I met someone." Brad exhaled. "She's in my running group."

"Did you cheat on me?" Nora asked before she'd thought better of it. She didn't really want to know the answer.

"No! No. I wouldn't do that," Brad said. "I just. . . meeting her, it made me rethink our relationship. I just. . . I don't know if we have anything in common, Nora. We're such different people. And Clair—she gets me. She's a partner at an advertising firm, she runs marathons—she's running tomorrow in the Twin Cities Marathon. She's just more like—"

Nora lifted her palm toward Brad, "Stop—I've heard enough." Nora paused, dropped her hand by her side, and took a deep breath. "Okay. . . okay. If you really feel that way, we've got some things to sort out."

"Yeah, about that. Do you think you could give me your ring back? I'm hoping I can return it," he said.

All of the fight drained out of Nora. "Yeah, no problem," she said, pulling the ring off her finger and laying it on Brad's glass-top coffee table. Nora picked up her purse, walked to the front door, and pushed down the handle. Without looking toward Brad she said, "Enjoy New York. *I hope you fall on your face.*" Brad didn't hear the last seven words because Nora hadn't said them aloud. The heavy condo door closed behind her.

Nora sat in her parked car outside Brad's condo building and tried to catch her breath between the gasping sobs that had overtaken her once she got outside. Deep down—or maybe not so deep down—she'd known this was coming, but she still hadn't been prepared for the reality of it. She'd thought Brad was the one. *The third time's the charm, right?* And for years they'd been happy, really happy. Or at least Nora thought they had been.

About six months after the breakup with David and her move from New York back to the Twin Cities, Nora had started half-heartedly online dating. Melanie had encouraged her, having met Mark through an app a few months earlier. Nora chatted with some men and even went on a couple dates before she decided it just wasn't for her. When she had opened the app one evening, intending to close her account, she saw that there was a message waiting in her inbox. Out of curiosity, she opened the message and saw that the good-looking advertising copywriter she'd matched with a few weeks prior had sent her a message. Nora and Brad spent the night exchanging messages, only going to sleep when they had set up a date for the next day.

The chemistry had been instant. Soon after that first date, Brad and Nora could barely stand to go a day without seeing each other. That initial rush had convinced Nora that this was it–she'd finally found the man she was supposed to marry. She quit her process of re-enrolling in graduate school in Illinois to stay in the Twin Cities with Brad because she was sure this—he—was going to be her forever. . .

Nora wiped her face on her sleeve and dug her cellphone out of her purse. There was only one person she wanted to talk to right now. The one person who had always known how to make the bad things better. He picked up on the third ring.

"Hello sweetheart! What's up?" said Jim, clearly having seen her name pop up on his caller ID.

"Daddy?" Nora sniffed into the phone, "Daddy, the wedding—he called it off."

ACT II

The Magic

CHAPTER 11 ~ SALLY

October 23, 2018

Bruce dumped his cold coffee in the sink and set the mug on the counter next to his dirty cereal bowl and spoon as Sally entered the kitchen in her robe.

"Sal, Tiff just left—said she'd be home 'bout the normal time. Which reminds me, I'm gonna be late tonight—another meeting about the Duluth branch."

"Okay," came Sally's emotionless response. "Should we wait to eat with you?"

"Nah, you guys do whatever—see you when I see you."

"Fine. . . bye." Sally walked out of the kitchen, knowing that Bruce would be gone before she returned. If anyone had been in the hallway leading to the laundry room, they would have seen her mouth *dickhead* when she heard the door open to the garage. Normally Sally didn't swear, not even to herself, but considering the circumstances, she'd been allowing herself to berate Bruce with minor profanities in her head. *Another late meeting, my ass. . . you. . . you. . . ass.*

It had been a week since Sally had seen Bruce in front of The St. Paul Hotel in the arms of the nubile redhead, and it appeared that Sally had been right about one thing—Bruce hadn't seen her. Either that, or he was a far better actor than Sally had ever given him credit for being. She still hadn't decided how to—or even if to—confront Bruce with her knowledge of his flagrant infidelity. Once Sally had quit crying over his betrayal and knew for sure that he wasn't going to broach the subject, she'd opted to give herself time to figure out what kind of future she wanted. She quickly discovered that what she thought she wanted changed from hour to hour: confront him, divorce him, win him back, kill him. All too often her thoughts landed on the final option.

Sally looked up from the piles of dirty clothes to the lucky kitty sitting on the laundry room windowsill. She reached over and flicked the cat's arm to make it wave faster. Seeing the waving figurine reminded her of the Lucky Dragon, which, in turn, reminded her that it was time to make a thrift store run. But she wasn't sure her heart was in the right place to do good deeds with the sentiment *kill him, kill him, kill him* caroming around in her head. It didn't seem like an altruistic refrain. She looked down at the soiled clothes and linens at her feet and began sorting the different colors into piles while she thought. . .

Murder. Sally knew she wouldn't go through with it— what would she do in a world without Bruce? They had been together for so long, almost thirty years, and Tiffany loved her father so much. There was no way she would do anything to upset Tiffany before she left for Spain. And, *damn him,* when she thought about her daughters' love for their dad, divorce didn't even seem like an option. Trudy thought of Bruce as her father; he was the only daddy she had ever known. Bruce had battled Sally's parents just as hard as Sally had to retain custody of Trudy when they'd married. By their first anniversary the custody wounds were healing, Bruce had made sure of that. Eventually, all was forgiven by her parents—they'd even grown to like Bruce. When her father was dying from chronic heart disease the year Sally turned thirty, her mother had admitted that it was a good thing that Sally and Bruce were raising Trudy, saying that she deserved parents young enough to see her all the way to adulthood. *Okay, I won't off the son of a biscuit. . .*

Sally pondered further. Could she survive in a world without Bruce? Well, financially, she could. She had money. Even with the huge amount she'd sunk into

Bruce's expanding business, she still had most of her inheritance. She'd always thought of that money as *theirs*, but that was pre-redhead. It had taken a week of indecision, but yesterday Sally had visited her financial advisor and made sure that all the newest accounts—the ones opened after her mother's death— were in her name only. She'd even changed all her beneficiary forms from Bruce's name to Trudy's. If she decided to leave, she wasn't going without what was left of her parents' money, and if she stayed, she was finally going to take control of her finances. *That's non-negotiable!*

She reached into the laundry hamper and yanked out one of Bruce's new dress shirts. She held it out, looked at it, and started to cry. Maybe she should just keep her mouth shut and go on as though she hadn't seen what she'd seen. Maybe it was her fault. Maybe she didn't pay enough attention to Bruce anymore. She certainly wasn't as pretty and slim as she had been when they'd first met. She glanced down at the sash of her faded bathrobe and groaned. She couldn't see past the knot tied at her ample waistline. Still, lots of women her age were heavy—it didn't justify an affair. *Why did he have to do this?* She pulled Bruce's shirt toward her wet eyes; the scent of an unfamiliar perfume wafted toward the ceiling. *Damn him.* Sally threw the shirt to the floor, wiped her eyes on the sleeve of her robe, and screamed in frustration toward the golden cat blithely waving to her from the windowsill. Once again, she started to think about the best ways to murder a sixty-year-old man to make it look like a household accident. *Oh stop it,* she thought, *he doesn't get to spoil my day. . .*

~

"You must be the lady that Bev told me about—the one who buys up all our yellow and red clothes," said the new volunteer running the cash register at Treasure Trove Thrift.

"I suppose I am. It's not likely there'd be two of us," Sally replied.

"What do you do with all this stuff? I mean, if it's okay to ask."

"Sure, I don't mind. I donate it by color to two other thrift stores. Have you ever noticed how much green clothing you have here? I buy up green clothes and linens at the other stores and donate all that stuff here. I call it my Thrift Store Color Distribution System or TSCDS for short."

"That's really nice of you. But, ya know it's kinda nutso, too, right?"

"Yeah, I know—that's probably why I like doing it. It makes me happy, and it doesn't hurt anyone, so I'm going to keep on being nutty," Sally said while raising her eyebrows and twirling her finger in front of her ear.

"Well, thanks. That'll be thirty-seven dollars."

Sally handed the bemused clerk a hundred-dollar bill, "Here. Keep the change for the women's shelter, and have a good day."

"Wow! Thanks, crazy lady!"

Giving away the money had made Sally feel happy—better than she'd felt since before last week's sighting of Bruce kissing the auburn-haired beauty. It felt good to Sally that she was out doing something she considered normal—even if, apparently, no one else did. How she wished the Lucky Dragon were still open. She could have stopped and had the lunch special—maybe even drowned her sorrows in an extra crab rangoon. She decided to drive by the closed Chinese restaurant for old times' sake—she really needed to check out the paint color again. Nora thinking that the building had been painted white still puzzled her.

Agog, Sally pulled into the parking lot beside the old restaurant. She parked and walked up to the front of the building. It was completely lavender now, except for the shutters, contrasting trim, and front door. Not only was it lavender, but it also now shimmered as though it had been coated with mica-flecked enamel. The window trim and door were a shade of deep forest green, and the wisteria was even more dazzling than Sally had remembered it from a week earlier. She touched one of the cascading blossoms. As impossible as it seemed, the plants were real. The deep purple and white flowers felt soft and warm in her hand. *This is bizarre,* thought Sally. *Maybe I am nutso. . .*

Sally pulled at the door handle. The door didn't budge. She walked to the window and tried to see inside, but gauzy curtains blocked her view. That's when she noticed a sign taped in the corner of the window that said: OPENING NEXT WEEK. *Wonderful,* thought Sally, *it's opening, whatever "it" is.* But, the *it* didn't matter; she knew she'd be back. She had to see inside the building—it was as though the exterior had been redecorated for her and her alone. *Will the interior follow suit?* she wondered.

Sally returned to her Sportage and tried to decide if she was ready to head back to St. Paul. She realized it was silly to blame Minneapolis's sister city for Bruce's indiscretion, but she kind of did. Maybe it was because the words "THE SAINT PAUL" were like a superscript on her internal video of that not-so-clandestine kiss now seared into her retinas. *No,* thought Sally, *I'm not going to be controlled by my emotions—he's not going to win this time.* She'd go to Twice Nice, shop for red and green things, drop off the yellow items she'd collected, and then hightail it for home. She wouldn't go near the hotel.

Turning out of the Lucky Dragon parking lot, Sally saw Nora across the street struggling to get a large hanger bag out of the back of her little blue car. *She must need to have some last-minute work done on her wedding dress,* thought Sally. If she remembered correctly, the wedding was later in the week. *Yes, Friday!* She recalled thinking that it was an odd day for a wedding. Sally didn't think that Nora looked happy—she hoped that nothing was seriously wrong with the dress. Nora didn't need that.

Seeing Nora reminded Sally that she still hadn't called Nora's mother about D'Wight's open house at Casket Arts. She'd call Deb after the big weekend. A little gallery shopping might be just what she and Deb needed to decompress after several trying weeks, albeit for very different reasons.

CHAPTER 12 ~ NORA

October 23, 2018

Nora's week following the breakup had been a whirlwind of canceling everything from the venue to the caterer, begging for deposits back, and having to tell far too many strangers her sob story. Brad hadn't been too involved in the wedding planning, and most of the expenses had gone on Nora's credit card, so it had all been up to her. All except the DJ, if he had actually booked one to begin with. Thankfully, she'd been spared telling most of the guests that the ceremony was off—Melanie had been a stellar matron of honor, calling everyone on the guest list to let them know. Nora's parents had been understanding and tried to comfort her, especially her father, but she could tell that they were disappointed—her mother in particular.

Her days had also been filled with crying. Lots of crying. Some of it was over the loss of the future she'd pictured with Brad, but much of it was just about, well, her. This was the third man who had changed his mind about marrying her. *What is wrong with me? Am I cursed?*

Nora parked her car on the street outside The Little Wedding Shop. It was the final stop on her wedding canceling parade of indignities. She wrestled the overly large garment bag out of the back of her little Civic, almost falling into a leaf-strewn puddle in the process. Shoving the garment bag through the front door, she was once again greeted by the smiley blonde Chloe. *Doesn't anyone else work here?*

"Oh, you're back! Do you have a last-minute alteration?" she asked, coming out from behind the counter.

"Um, no. I was actually wondering if I could return this," Nora said with a sigh in her voice.

"Oh, did you find something else?" Chloe asked, cocking her head to the side. "I really thought this dress was perfect for you."

"No, I'm. . . no longer getting married," Nora admitted.

"Oh, I'm so sorry. . . Unfortunately, because your dress was made to order, we have a no return policy," Chloe said looking deeply uncomfortable.

"Of course," Nora said, closing her eyes, and pinching the bridge of her nose with her free hand, attempting to prevent the tears from starting again.

"I'm really, really sorry," Chloe said. She sounded as though she meant it. "You could try selling it online. It's really a beautiful dress. Or, you could keep it for your future wedding."

"Future wedding. Right. Well, thanks anyway," Nora said, turning back to the door, her eyes filling with tears.

"Good luck!" Chloe called out to Nora's back as she struggled out the door with her dress still in tow.

Luck. Nora felt like that was something that had always been in short supply for her. The thought made tears start to fall as she trudged back to her car, barely keeping the dress bag off the ground. As she shoved the dress in her back seat, the gleaming white walls of the former Lucky Dragon restaurant caught her eye. It seemed to sparkle despite the dreary day. The green ferns in the black window boxes appeared to have grown since she last saw them—*they must be real.* Nora wiped the tears from her cheeks with the back of her hand, finished shoving the dress in the back seat, and locked the car again. She walked over to the building to inspect the ferns. At the window box beside the front door, she touched the leaves–they were indeed real. *How odd,* she thought. *Well, they won't last much longer, the forecast calls for freezing temperatures later this week.*

There was a sign on the door saying, OPEN—PLEASE COME IN. Nora sniffled and wiped her face again, this time with her sleeve, and reached for the door. She needed to know what this place was that had so quickly taken over D'Wight's restaurant.

As soon as Nora touched the door handle, it swung wide. She heard a little bell tinkle overhead as she stepped in, and the door shut behind her as though caught by a brisk wind. She could barely believe her eyes. In only a few short weeks, the restaurant had been gutted and replaced by the most glorious bookshop that Nora had ever seen. The interior was filled with antique wood shelves, brimming with many of Nora's favorite books and others she was dying to read. Amid the shelves, cozy nooks with overstuffed armchairs and soft blankets invited would-be-patrons to sit and read. There was even a beautiful calico cat curled up on the armchair closest to the fireplace. A cheerful fire crackled in the grate, warming the room. The air was scented with wood smoke, new books, and the faint trace of an expensive cigar.

Nora walked closer to the fire. She scratched the cat's head, and it began to purr. She'd always been a sucker for a bookstore cat. *This place is like a dream come true,* Nora thought.

"That's because it is, Nora," came a deep voice from behind her. Nora whirled around. There was no one there.

"Hel. . . Hello?" said Nora, peering around the shelf closest to her where she thought the voice had come from. Still, no one was there. *Am I losing it? Has this breakup finally driven me crazy?*

"No, you aren't crazy, Nora," said the same voice, this time coming from the opposite corner of the room.

"Replying to my thoughts isn't exactly helping your case," Nora said aloud, turning around in a circle.

"I suppose it isn't," said the voice. "Let's just continue to speak aloud then, shall we?"

"Who are you?" Nora asked, still gazing around the room, looking for the owner of the voice.

"I'm the Lucky Dragon, of course. My name is on the outside of the building, is it not?"

"They took that down," Nora said absently, thinking of the sign with the dice-rolling and cigar-smoking dragon that used to grace the outside of the restaurant. Then, she remembered she was speaking to a disembodied voice that seemed to be able to read her mind. "Wait, who are you, really?"

At the question, the fire in the fireplace grate and all the sconces around the room (which Nora had assumed were fake—just those flickering flame-shaped light bulbs) burst upward, producing a few dazzling seconds of light and heat before returning to their former sedate level. Nora stumbled back from the fire, catching herself on an endcap-table displaying some of her favorite YA books from her teen years.

"Okay," she said, her voice trembling. "You're a dragon."

"Not just any dragon, I'm the Lucky Dragon," the room replied.

"What do you want with me?" Nora said, slinking backward toward the door. She needed to get out of this place. *Does D'Wight know the new owner thinks he's a dragon?*

"Not so fast," said the Lucky Dragon as Nora heard a click come from the door. He'd locked her in. Nora quickly turned and looked at the door. She didn't see any way to spring the newly locked deadbolt. Her heart began to race at the thought of being trapped in the building with this. . . *Person? Spirit? Dragon?* She wasn't entirely sure.

"I'll let you go very soon, but first we need to have a little chat. Please, have a seat by the fire," the Lucky Dragon said.

Nora slowly turned around. The chair where the cat had been sleeping was empty. A hot cup of coffee—she could see the steam rising from the mug—now sat on the table beside the chair along with a small cream pitcher and a plate of oatmeal cookies with chunks of white chocolate and dried cranberries. They looked just like the ones from her favorite Urbana, Illinois bakery—the one just down the street from where she'd lived in grad school. A little place-card beside the coffee mug said "Nora" in curly script.

"How did you do that?" Nora asked, her amazement making her forget to be afraid. She walked towards the chair to examine the treats.

"I can do a myriad of things, Nora. Please, sit and I'll tell you more."

Not knowing what else to do, Nora did as she was told and sat down, picking up one of the cookies to examine it.

"Feel free to take a bite. I know they're your favorite," said the Lucky Dragon.

Nora remembered her mother's warnings from when she was younger to not accept food from strange men. Although Deb had likely meant possible kidnappers driving panel vans, Nora thought the Lucky Dragon definitely counted as a strange man, even if he wasn't technically a man. She set the delicious looking cookie back on the plate.

"Nora, you have been chosen to have three wishes granted. Think of me as your genie and this building as my magic lamp. These aren't just any wishes, however. You may only wish for something that you have already had."

"What do you mean?" Nora asked, not believing that she was actually a participant in this bizarre conversation.

"Think of the things that you've had in your life that you desperately want back. Those things, and only those things, are what you are able to wish for."

Nora could think of a lot of things that she'd once had that she didn't have anymore: the potential for a career in library science, her best friend's time, her parent's approval, and, of course, her engagement to Brad.

"I know what I want," Nora said quickly, still not believing that she was talking to a. . . dragon. . . a dragon building?

"Good things come to those who wait, Nora. Besides, you don't know the price yet," the dragon said. "Fools rush in where angels fear to tread."

"The price?" Nora asked, looking about the room, still not sure where to direct her gaze.

"Magic always requires payment, Nora. There's no such thing as a free lunch," said the Lucky Dragon. "To receive the peak, you must experience the valley. For each wish to be granted, you will be made to endure the worst experience of your life, even if it hasn't happened yet. The event will be equal to your wish in its scope. As you are so young, many of your worst days are yet ahead of you."

"A comforting thought," Nora grumbled.

The Lucky Dragon continued, ignoring her comment. "I will pick something from your past or your future as it currently appears. When experiencing it, you won't know that it is only to last a day. The pain, be it physical or emotional, will be real. But remember, futures can always change."

"So, each payment is only like a day, but the fulfilled wish will last forever?" Nora asked, thinking that she had the better end of the bargain.

"Yes, but you won't know that the experience is a payment. It will feel as though it is actually happening, and it may actually happen in the future," the dragon said. "The fear of not knowing can be worse than the experience itself."

Nora still thought the wishes—if any of this was true and she wasn't having a psychological break—seemed like a good deal.

"You cannot make the wishes now. You must go home and think about this. You should return in two weeks' time with your answer and, if you so choose, your first wish. Just make sure that what you wish for is worth the price you will pay."

With that, the fire in the hearth died and the front door unbolted and sprung open. Nora, clearly understanding that she was being dismissed, got up from the chair and hurried to the door, eager to get away from this lovely place that was making her question her sanity.

Nora had just stepped out the door when she heard the Lucky Dragon speak one more time. "So, remember, Nora. Be careful what you wish for. . ." With that, the door slammed shut.

CHAPTER 13 ~ SALLY

The next week, during Sally's thrift store circuit, the sign in the window of the old Lucky Dragon that had read, OPENING NEXT WEEK, was gone. A new sign on the front door said: OPEN—PLEASE COME IN.

A light snow fell, covering the delicate wisteria blossoms. Sally shook her head at the unbelievable sight as she reached for the door handle. Before she could push on it, the door swung on its hinges as if aided by a force inside the building. It was as though someone—or something— had wanted to pull Sally into the remodeled interior. The door automatically closed behind Sally, and, though she didn't take notice, the bolt to the old-fashioned night-lock slid into place, and the OPEN sign vanished from the door's window.

Sally brushed powdery snowflakes from her hair and off the shoulders of her peacoat onto the floral rug that graced the entry before she walked any further into the beautifully appointed teashop. The charm of the interior matched that of the building's exterior. It could not have been more perfect in Sally's eyes: a mix of small round and square tables covered by white damask tablecloths, each table accompanied by two or four dainty gold Chippendale chairs; two deep green velvet couches faced one another flanking a glowing fireplace; a large ornate coffee table sat between the couches with a centerpiece of fresh flowers and an assortment of glossy books about art and architecture. Lining the teashop walls, antique sideboards held tiered porcelain trays and colorful teapots, and tall bookcases stood with their shelves bowed by the weight of more books, pots, and plates.

Toward the center of the room sat a small round table. It was set with accoutrements for tea and displayed a formal place card. On it was written, "Sally."

Sally looked at the beautifully laid table and thought, *can this possibly be for me?*

"Who else would it be for?" came a disembodied voice from across the room.

Sally jumped. "Where are you?" she asked, speaking in the direction of the voice.

"Over here," came the voice, now from the opposite side of the room.

Now you're just messing with me, thought Sally.

"You are discerning," said the smooth low voice from overhead, punctuated by a rumbling chuckle.

"Who are you?" asked Sally loudly, her voice echoing through the teashop.

"Thank you for speaking up—I do prefer that. You may think of me as the Lucky Dragon," came the reply.

I'm losing everything—first my husband, now my mind. This is crazy. Sally cleared her throat and spoke. "Why can't I see you?"

"No, Sally, you're not going crazy, and you can't see me because I'm a dragon. Have you ever heard the expression, 'like a bull in a china shop?' Well, you haven't seen anything until you've witnessed a two-thousand-pound dragon flying around a teashop. Besides, I'm told I smell like cigars. I smoke fine cigars, but people complain, nonetheless," the dragon said, a hint of resignation in his deep voice.

"Well, okay, but I have another question. Why is my name on this card? Were you expecting me?" Sally asked.

Suddenly, the chair closest to the place card slid out from the table. "Take your seat, and pour yourself a 'cuppa,' as the Brits say, and I'll explain everything," said the voice now coming from the chair across from where Sally had been invited to sit.

An hour later, Sally walked out the door of the refurbished Lucky Dragon with more questions than she'd had when she'd entered the building. She still posited that she might be losing her mind as she pondered all that the dragon had told her: it seemed that Sally had been chosen—by whom was still unclear to her—to have three wishes granted. The wishes were not just any wishes, but had to be the reoccurrence of something from Sally's past. For example, she couldn't wish for a trillion dollars, because she had never possessed a trillion dollars. She could, however, wish to be as monetarily wealthy as she had ever been—but in her case that would be a waste of a wish since Sally was currently nearly as rich as she had ever been. Also, the wishes could only be for and about herself. For instance, she could not wish for Bruce to love her as much as he once had. She could, however, wish to love Bruce as much as she once had, which, under their present circumstances, seemed like a cruel thing to do to herself; it was better to know Bruce's foibles and be able to look at him through thoroughly un-rose-tinted glasses—especially, if he was getting ready to leave her.

The Lucky Dragon had explained further that the wishes came with a hitch. The dragon, who tended to speak in old saws and mixed metaphors, said, "You understand, Sally, even in the metaphysical world, there's no such thing as a free lunch. You are going to have to pay the piper."

He told Sally that for each wish she was granted, she would have to relive hours of the worst times in her life. The real kicker was that she could not choose those times. The horrible events and their aftermaths would be chosen for her, and they would be commensurate with her desire for the wish, i.e., Sally's 'number one' wish would be paid for by her enduring hours of her absolute worst day. And to top it off, the dragon had explained, the physical and emotional pains would be fresh and raw; Sally would not realize that it was an event from her past and would be over within hours. If she were to choose a wish, she would willingly be placing herself back into the quagmire of her worst lived nightmares.

The dragon let Sally know that she had time to consider the offer. He suggested she go home and think about what three things from her earlier life she would like to regain and, also, what pains she might have to endure to have her wishes come true. Lucky D, as she had begun to think of the dragon, had suggested that Sally not start with her biggest wish—he said that it would be a good idea to proceed with care when deciding whether the gain would be worth the pain.

"Go home and sleep on it. When you come back next week, you'll know what you want to do," Lucky D said, upon which Sally's chair was pulled away from the tea table by an invisible server, and the front door of the teashop unlocked and swung open without apparent assistance.

~

Ha! Sleep on it, thought Sally as she kicked at the sheet wrapped around her left leg. It wasn't as if sleep had come easily for her in the weeks since she'd found out that Bruce was cheating, *and now this, whatever this is. At least,* thought Sally, *I'm not frightened by the dragon.* She was, however, frighted by reliving things from her past, and those were the things keeping her awake. Sally got up from the king-size bed that she and Bruce had been sharing since moving into their Edina home. She straightened the sheets. The clock read 1:17 a.m.—Bruce wasn't home. Sally assumed he was with his *friend.* She needed to come-up with a better name for Bruce's paramour, but it wasn't going to be *paramour*—that was too pretty a word. Perhaps, *skank, trollop, floozy.* No, Sally wouldn't allow herself to even think those words. Bruce was lying to her, maybe he was lying to the redhead as well. Yeah, maybe the *skank, trollop, floozy* just thinks she's dating a busy sixty-year-old man with no baggage. *Sure, that's it. . . sure it is. . . ha!*

Sally used the bathroom and climbed back into bed. Instead of thinking about Bruce or their past, she began pondering what she might like to change about herself. If she really got to change three things, what would they be? And, in what order? She remembered the Lucky Dragon saying that she should not start with her top desire because the payment might be more than she would want to relive. Sally knew that would be true—she'd learned early in life about both physical and emotional pain—*but, I need to choose three things to change before I can make up my mind, right?* Well, her greatest personal wish for years had been to have her slim figure back; that would have to be her top wish. As for the other two, maybe she would wish to feel as good physically as she ever had. *Oh, to feel like I did when I was in high school—before the accident tore my life and body to pieces.* Thoughts of high school brought back memories of meeting Bentley Bradley, the cute boy with two last names. The longer she thought about Ben, the more she could feel his arms as he'd slid them beneath her coat on the night he'd taken her home after his college's winter formal. She felt the euphoria she had experienced that cold evening when he'd kissed her for the first time. It was as though their feet had left the porch steps at the front of her parent's grand house, and she and Ben had floated through the starlit sky like a couple in a Chagall painting.

Sally barely stirred an hour later when Bruce quietly slipped into his side of their bed, smelling of his friend's perfume.

~

Friday. Nora's getting married today, thought Sally as she wound the cord around the large plastic hooks on the back of the upright vacuum. *Ahh, young love. . . but Nora's not so young. She must be about Trudy's age—mid thirties? Still young, just not impetuous. She must be so happy and excited. . . I'll get a full report when I call Deb next week.*

Sally put the vacuum back in the hall closet and then went to the cabinet under the kitchen sink to grab the Pledge and a dust rag. She had always done the family's housework to save money. After their move to the Cities, Sally had considered looking for a cleaning service, but since she wasn't working, Bruce had said he still thought it a waste of money—Sally could keep the house clean. He had added, "you could use the exercise"— five little words that Sally had tried to forget but couldn't. They were like a knife stuck in her solar plexus that twisted with every other unkind comment that spilled from Bruce's mouth. *Bruce, what to do about Bruce. . .*

Entering the living room, Sally sprayed Pledge on the clean dust rag. She always wiped the mid-size grand piano first. A gift from her parents when she'd turned sixteen, it was the most expensive piece of furniture she owned, and she didn't want to risk scratching it with a dirty rag. *Furniture*, that's how she thought about the instrument now that no one had played it since Tiffany had quit lessons the year she'd entered middle school. Trudy had been a good pianist, so maybe, once she and Enrique settled somewhere permanently, she would want the heirloom instrument for herself and the boys.

Sally dusted the top of the piano and then pulled the bench from beneath the keyboard and gave it a cursory swipe before sitting down, adjusting her position, and opening the fallboard. She placed her righthand at middle C and clumsily played a scale. To think that she was once considered the best young pianist in the Midwest. She remembered the accolades and the applause, but most of all she remembered the feeling of sitting down at this very piano and playing whatever came into her mind. Her emotions would fill her parents' living room—notes bouncing off the walls when she was angry, crawling beneath the carpets when she was sad. Ben had loved the way she played and promised Sally that if her parents wouldn't let her take her piano, they would buy one just as soon as they could manage the expense. Sally lowered the fallboard. She hadn't been able to play since the accident. When relearning skills, piano performance hadn't seemed a priority—holding a fork, learning to read, and walking had all taken precedence. She'd learned to live without the piano, but still missed it. *Maybe being able to play again should be my wish,* thought Sally. *It's not as important as my first two wishes, but it would be so nice to be able to lose myself in music again. . . I'll wish to play like I did when I was seventeen. . .*

Sally sprayed more Pledge on the rag and continued dusting the furniture in the living room.

CHAPTER 14 ~ NORA

On October twenty-sixth, her would-have-been wedding day, Nora didn't get out of bed. Or at least she hadn't planned to get out of bed. As she was watching an old *Parks and Recreation* episode on her laptop and eating peanut butter straight from the jar, her front door unlocked and opened. It startled Nora so much that the computer slipped from her lap, and she threw the peanut butter slathered spoon in the air. It landed in the unruly tufts of her zebra-striped rug.

"Don't worry, it's just me!" came the shout from the door as Melanie entered carrying a grocery bag and bottle of wine. "Time to get up, sleepyhead!" Melanie walked to the kitchen and set the bag and wine on Nora's table. She then opened the window blinds around the studio apartment that had been blocking the late-morning sun from brightening the L-shaped room.

"How did you get in?" Nora said, hitting the spacebar on her retrieved laptop to pause the sitcom and rubbing her eyes.

"I used my emergency key—you gave me a copy when you moved in, remember?" Melanie started pulling food out of the grocery bag and putting it in the fridge. "We have a full day ahead of us. Put down your laptop and peanut butter, pick up your spoon, and go get in the shower."

Nora sat on the edge of the bed, still confused as to what was happening. "Where's Juliet?" Nora couldn't remember the last time she'd spent time with her friend without her daughter around.

"She's with Mark's parents today. It's just you and me, Bunny," Melanie said, picking up the coffee pot and pouring the remains of the burnt-smelling brew in the sink. "First things first—as soon as you're clean and dressed, we're going to get real coffee."

A half-hour later, the two women left Nora's apartment, taking Melanie's car to Isles Bun and Coffee for pumpkin-spiced lattes, breakfast sandwiches, and a dessert of long, twisted cinnamon rolls called Puppy Dog Tails. They followed their late breakfast with a trip to Nora's favorite bookstore, Magers and Quinn, and Melanie bought her a new collectors edition of the best breakup book that either of them could think of—*Ethan Frome* by Edith Wharton. "Nothing says 'romance is dead' like a man leaving his wife for her younger cousin and immediately getting in a debilitating sledding accident," joked Melanie while handing over her credit card to the cashier.

Following the bookstore trip, Melanie drove to the Minneapolis Institute of Art, one of their favorite places to walk around and talk when they were in their early twenties—primarily because viewing the art was always free and they were always broke. This day, without discussing it, Nora and Melanie took the wide, airy stairway to the third floor and started down the hallway toward the Impressionists wing, always a favorite area of the museum for them both. Reaching the Monets and Renoirs, they slowed to look at the paintings.

"Did you know this is where I took Brad on one of our first dates?" Nora said. The date had been Nora's idea. Their first date had been drinks, that turned into dinner, that turned into dessert. The second date had been more of the same. It had been lovely, but Nora was concerned that Brad—who insisted on paying for all of it—had spent too much money on her in the short time they'd been together. To remedy that, she had suggested a walk around the art institute. He had obliged, and Nora had thought it sweet when he'd let her give him a two-and-a-half-hour tour of her favorite exhibits and pieces. He'd asked her questions and pointed out the things he liked, despite saying he didn't know much about art other than what he had been taught by the graphic designers at his advertising firm. They had returned to the art institute a couple of times in their first years of dating, but Nora now couldn't recall the last time Brad had accompanied her here, or to any museum or gallery for that matter. . .

"Oh, I'm sorry, I should have remembered you and Br. . . we can go somewhere else," Melanie said, a look of horror on her face.

"No, no. I don't want to go. This was our place first—I won't let him take that from us." Nora linked arms with her friend and tried to ignore the ache in her chest that arose with thoughts of Brad during the years when he was truly hers.

Following more gallery wandering, Nora and Melanie returned to Nora's apartment where Melanie poured them each a glass of white wine, started playing a Taylor Swift playlist from her iPhone, and got busy preparing a dinner of pasta carbonara. Despite working at an Italian restaurant, Nora still favored Melanie's version of the dish; she added peas—Nora's favorite vegetable—and replaced the pancetta with thick-cut bacon. Melanie made Nora sit at the table with her glass of wine, insisting that the kitchen in the little apartment was only big enough for one person at a time. After singing their hearts out to Blank Space, Melanie set two bowls of pasta on the dining table and topped up Nora's wine glass. As Melanie settled in, Nora reached over and grabbed her hand.

"Hey, this day was amazing. Thank you for being so great about. . . everything," Nora said, her eyes welling with tears. "I still can't believe you called the entire guest list to let them know. . ."

"Hey, no crying! We were doing so well!" Melanie said, clutching Nora's hand tighter. "And, it was the least I could do."

"These are mostly happy tears, I promise," Nora said, using her free hand to wipe her eyes. "I'm just so lucky to have you in my life, that's all. And I guess . . . well, I've missed you."

"Oh, Bunny, I know things are different now, but you'll always be my best friend," Melanie smiled and gave Nora's hand one last squeeze before letting go. "Now, let's eat before it gets cold."

Melanie, needing to pick up Juliet at her in-laws' place, left shortly after washing the dinner dishes. Nora, now alone, sat in the dark and thought about what she should have been doing at that moment. She imagined her family and friends watching her as she and Brad had their first dance in the window-lined room at the Van Dusen Mansion. She should have been wearing her gorgeous wedding gown right now. Instead, that gown now seemed to be mocking her, sticking out of her tiny closet. *No, Wanamaker, think of something else! Do not cry!*

To distract herself, she thought about the weird experience she'd had the previous day at the old Lucky Dragon restaurant. At several points during their afternoon, she'd considered telling Melanie about the magical bookstore and the disembodied voice saying it would grant her three wishes, but she couldn't figure out a way to bring it up that didn't sound like she'd had a major psychological break. And, honestly, she still wasn't sure that wasn't the case.

Cold, Nora got into her bed with her laptop and the rest of the bottle of wine Melanie had left with her. "I think I need to start seeing a therapist," Nora muttered to herself. After taking a swig of wine right from the bottle, she typed in the web address for her health insurance company to see if they covered mental health care. Unfortunately, even this mundane task made her think of Brad—he had better insurance than she did, and she'd planned on switching to his after the wedding. After floundering through the fine print of the policy only to determine that the coverage for mental health issues was next to nonexistent, she closed her computer and set it, along with the now-empty wine bottle, on her bedside table. She pulled her comforter to her chin as the ancient radiator clanked and hissed on the other side of her tiny apartment. *Everything about Brad's life is better,* she thought, *and it was going to be my life. . . but maybe with the dragon's help it still can be. . . maybe. . . maybe. . . maybe. . .*

Counting "maybes" like sheep, Nora drifted off to sleep.

CHAPTER 15 ~ SALLY

"Hello, Wanamakers," came Deb's phone greeting, a habit from her many years of answering the family's landline.

"Hi, Deb. This is Sally Munson, Nora's friend—we met at the Lucky Dragon sale."

"Oh, sure. I remember." Sally heard Deb set something down; she assumed it was her coffee cup.

"I said I'd call about the open house at the Casket Arts Building this weekend. I know it's short notice now, but I wanted to wait until after Nora's wedding. I figured as the mother of the bride you'd be swamped."

"So, you haven't heard," Deb huffed.

"What?— Is everything okay?" Sally said as she clutched her phone tighter, inadvertently making it beep.

"Nora botched another one."

"Pardon?" Sally said, trying to imagine what her young friend could have done.

"The wedding didn't happen. Nora's fiancé called it off."

"Oh, Deb, I'm so sorry for Nora."

"Well, yes, but it's not like she hasn't gone through it before. This is her third broken engagement. I'm the one who's disappointed—I thought it was really going to happen this time."

"I'm sure Nora's got to be devastated."

"She was at first, but I think now she's just mad. She spent—we spent—a lot of money for nothing."

"Would you mind giving me Nora's number? I mean, if you think it would be okay. I'd like to call her with my condolences—um, I'm not sure if that's the right word— I'd just like to call her."

"You don't have her number?"

"No, we hadn't gotten that far along in our friendship. Do you think she would mind if I called?" Sally rummaged in vain for a pen that worked from the mug at the end of the kitchen counter as Deb kept talking.

"No—she just won't answer if she doesn't want to talk. She barely ever answers the phone when I call. Maybe you should text her first."

"Okay, I'll do that—just text me her number." Sally paused, then said, "So, do you still want to go to D'Wight's open house?"

"Sure. And, if you call her, you might want to see if Nora would want to join us. I don't imagine she's got much going on right now."

Ouch, thought Sally, but said, "I'll give you a call to set up a time after I text Nora."

"Great—bye."

"Bye, Deb," Sally said into the dead phone, not realizing Deb had already hung up. Sally laid her phone on the kitchen counter and scooped up the pile of dried-up pens to deposit in the trash. *Poor Nora. Three broken engagements— what that must do to a person's self-esteem. Deb didn't seem very understanding, but then I don't know what it's like to help a daughter plan three weddings that never happen. Still, she could be kinder. . . no, no, no—just stay out of it.* Sally thought about how she'd feel if someone got in the middle of one of her frequent spats with Tiffany—*It doesn't mean that they don't love each other.*

~

Sally greeted Nora and Deb at the entrance to the Casket Arts Building after which Deb spoke first, "It's nice of you to offer to drive Nora home—I hadn't planned on needing to leave the open house so early, but if I want to keep my place as a mahjong alternate, I have to show up when I get called. Besides, I sense this is more yours and Nora's kinda thing than it is mine."

"It's no problem. I'm sure you'll enjoy seeing the artwork in the time you have." Sally said.

"Eh, I wouldn't count on it—it looks a bit hippy-dippy to me. Besides, my walls are full of pretty things from Home Interiors. Do you remember that company, Sally? Their pictures are really more to my taste," Deb said as she opened the heavy door and walked into the old industrial building.

"Oh, sure. I got rid of a lot of their stuff when we moved, but I think my entry mirror came from a party. I remember the catalogues being passed around the office. It seemed like someone knew someone having some kind of in-home sales party every week back in the eighties."

"Remember Tupperware?" Deb asked.

"Everyone remembers Tupperware, Mom—I think it's still around, though you're far more likely to get invited to a Pampered Chef party these days."

"Yeah. Didn't one of your friends want to have a Pampered Chef wedding shower for you? Glad that didn't pan out—you'd have even more stuff to return to people," Deb said, completely oblivious to the withering look her comment had elicited from her daughter as the three women walked down a wide hallway.

Sally, wishing to change the subject, said, "Let's head up these stairs—I'm pretty sure that D'Wight's studio is on the second floor." At the top of the stairs, she stopped and said, "Would you look at that!" when they'd encountered a multi-color, seven-foot rabbit.

"See? Now where would a person in her right mind put something like that?" Deb responded.

"I get your point—but don't you think it's fantastic? I love the colors, and it's just so whimsical," Sally said.

Sally's diversionary tactics had accomplished what she'd hoped and given Nora time to compose herself by the time the trio reached D'Wight's studio.

"Hello! You made it!" came D'Wight's greeting when he saw Sally and Deb walk through his door. He was wearing a black turtleneck and large, black-framed glasses.

"Hey, D'Wight! Don't you look like an *artiste*. I didn't even know you wore glasses," Sally said.

D'Wight barely heard her comment he was so distracted looking at Nora standing behind the two older women. "Oh these," he said as he shook his head. He stuck his finger through the glassless frames. "I just thought they made me look the part."

"Guess you were right," Nora said stepping forward.

"Hi, Nora. I didn't expect to see you—I thought you'd be off on your honeymoon."

Nora shrugged, "Seems I'm still in town."

"I hope nothing's wrong—your husband's not sick, is he? It'd suck to get sick and miss your own honeymoon."

"Nope, Brad isn't sick—he's just not my husband. We didn't get married," Nora said.

At that, Deb interjected, "No marriage, no honeymoon—at least we hadn't paid for that already."

"Mom, please. . ."

"Maybe it's for the best," D'Wight said.

"What?!" replied an incredulous Deb.

"Uh, it's just something people say—sorry," D'Wight looked around the room for a way to change the subject. Gesturing at the buffet table he continued, "Please, help yourself to some Chinese inspired tidbits—it's an assortment of my mom's favorites. Of course, not as good as hers, but not half bad if I do say so myself."

Sally had been busy looking around the studio while D'Wight tried to extract his foot from his mouth with his pu pu platter diversion. As Deb searched for the smallest egg roll, then, once found, dabbed at it with a napkin, Sally said, "D'Wight, your work is amazing! I can't believe the size of some of these pieces. Do you call them sculptures?"

"I usually refer to them as origami assemblages."

"Who would buy them? They're so big—just like that rabbit in the hallway. Who buys this kinda stuff?" Deb asked.

"Lots of people have big blank walls," D'Wight countered. "I've placed some in loft apartments, even a few in McMansion stairwells and three-story entryways—but mostly I sell them as commercial or public art. The curators at big clinics and hospitals like crane assemblages. In China, the crane is associated with longevity and wisdom—it kind of makes them perfect for places where healing's going on; patients want longevity and doctors want wisdom—or maybe the patients want wise doctors."

"I think they're beautiful, D'Wight," Nora said. "I want you to know that I'm sorry for never getting back to you on your offer to help with my wedding deco—"

"It's good you didn't, you'd just have another bill," interjected Deb.

Nora looked at her mom and shook her head, her lips smashed together, her mouth in a grim straight line.

"Oh, I wouldn't have charged Nora anything. It would have been my pleasure. In fact, Nora, if you still have all the cranes you made, maybe I can help you create a different work of art with them—a smaller assemblage piece, or a mobile, like the one over there." D'Wight pointed toward the ceiling in front of one of the big windows lining his studio. "Even if you don't have wall space, most folks have room to hang something from their ceiling."

Before Nora had a chance to respond, Deb said, "Well, this has been really interesting, but I've got to get to my mahjong group. I hope things work out for you here."

"Oh, I'm sorry you all have to go so soon," D'Wight said.

"We don't. Just my mom. Sally and I are just getting started," Nora said while she escorted Deb toward the open door. "Bye, Mom. I'll call you next week."

As Deb was leaving the studio, another guest arrived, and D'Wight got busy hosting—a skill he'd honed during his years of greeting people at the Lucky Dragon. When he finally managed to return to Nora and Sally, he asked, "So what do you think, Nora? Do you want to work on a project with me?"

"I'd love that, but can we wait a little while? I'm not sure I can handle it right now—it's sorta too soon for me to think about those cranes, if you know what I mean. Maybe early next year? I can give you my number if you want to text me—I imagine you're pretty busy right now, anyway."

"Never too busy for a friend—but, yeah, I get that it might be too soon. Sorry if what I said was insensitive," D'Wight passed Nora his phone. She typed in her number and handed the phone back to D'Wight who was biting his lower lip to suppress a grin.

"D'Wight, what do you think of the changes being made to the Lucky Dragon building?" Sally asked. "You still live above the restaurant, right?"

"Yeah, I do. I'm just really surprised that the new owners haven't started working on the exterior—I woulda thought they would've at least painted the trim before the snow started, but then, I know very little about construction—and I got paid for the building—so I'm not asking questions."

Sally looked from D'Wight to Nora, who looked as bewildered as Sally felt. Sally shrugged and said to D'Wight, "Yeah, best let sleeping dragons lie."

"You're funny," D'Wight responded. "I like funny people."

Sally and Nora said their goodbyes to D'Wight, and as soon as they were out of his earshot, Nora turned to Sally, "What do you make of D'Wight not thinking any changes have been made to the Lucky Dragon? Do you still think that the building's been painted lavender?"

"Yes, lavender with green trim. I'm sure of it," Sally said as they walked down the long second floor hallway at Casket Arts.

"But, it's not—it's been painted, but it's white with black trim. I was just there—it's very farmhouse chic."

Sally shook her head and looked puzzled. "Have you been inside?"

"Yeah—it's a great little bookstore—the kind I'd like to work at if it weren't for some very odd things."

"Odd—I get that... but for me it's a charming teashop."

"I'm really glad my mom couldn't stick around, because we need to talk. There's something very weird going on. My shift at Gina's doesn't start until 5:00—would you have time for a drink?" Nora asked. "I want to tell you something, and I need to be seated when you tell me I'm out of my mind."

~

Sally and Nora took seats at a small table toward the far end of the banquette wall at Northeast Social. With its magical smoky-blue walls, copper cornices, and spooky portraits of hollow-eyed long-necked men and women, Sally thought it must have made a perfect venue for a Halloween party. However, when she spied the pile of Christmas decorations in the corner beside their table, she knew the neighborhood café would undoubtedly have a different vibe in a few days.

After placing their order with the affable, multi-pierced server, Nora began to tell Sally about what she'd seen and heard at the old Chinese restaurant, ". . . so, anyway, like I don't know what I should wish for from. . . him? I don't even know who I'm talking to except it's a masculine voice. . . this is all so crazy."

"Well, if you're heading to Crazyville, Google Maps has us on the same route. Except in my version the building— which is now a teashop—is painted lavender, and I called the disembodied, grumbly voice Lucky Dragon, or Lucky D—or, sometimes, LD—which he seemed to like. He's granting me three wishes, too, but I think what we're being offered is a little different. I get to wish for something that I had in my past—like good health or a good figure; I can't make anyone else change, and I have to pay by reliving the absolute worst things I've already experienced, which I'm not sure I'm ready to do."

"From the life you've already lived—your past—that's your deal?"

"Yup—the wishes are from my past and so are my payments. Your offer is different, right?" Sally asked.

Once again, Nora explained to Sally that the voice, or Lucky D to use one of Sally's nicknames for the voice, had told her to think of things or people that she'd had in her life that she desperately wanted back. Lucky D had said that those things and people, and only those things and people, were what she could wish for. In payment for her three wishes, she would have to endure three of the worst experiences of her life—but not just those to date. Because Nora was so young, she would most likely have to pay with tragedies from her future. She explained to Sally that the wishes and payments were to be commensurate—in that respect, the offer was no different than the one proposed to Sally. Nora finished by saying, "I think I like the deal I'm being given more than the one the dragon's offered to you. You can just change things about yourself, right? I think, if I'm understanding my offer correctly, I can regain relationships—change the way people treat me. And, the payment? Well, I figure a person can put up with anything for a few hours."

"I don't think you're right about this at all," Sally said while tearing off a hunk of baguette that had just been dropped off by their server and spreading it with butter. "I'm not saying that you misunderstood Lucky D, but I think you're minimizing the payment that he's asking from you."

"How so?" Nora asked.

"First off, I'm not making light of your three broken engagements—they must have been awful for you—but I think that you are underestimating the horrors of the world—"

"But—"

"Please, let me finish," Sally said. "I know you think it's only going to be a few hours of pain for each wish, but that's not what I'm hearing. What I'm hearing is that you are most likely going to live through some dreadful things from your future. If you go along with the dragon on this, you're going see things—feel things—that you will never forget. If that happens, you'll wake up every day for the rest of your life expecting the worst."

"I think you worry too much, Sally." Nora took a sip of her Prosecco.

"You're not the first person to tell me that, but I still think I'm right to worry for you."

"Okay," Nora said, "give me some examples of what you think might happen to me. Prove to me that I'm wrong about this payment thing."

Sally looked around the dimly lit restaurant and, in a hushed voice, continued, "Well, I'm not going to be specific, but you could be in a terrible accident—or a fire. Or, maybe one day you'll have a child—or children—and something awful could happen to one or more of them. Having something bad happen to your child is undoubtedly the worst pain a parent can endure. Maybe the circumstances change, and the bad event doesn't occur. But, if it's really horrible, you'll never—I mean never—get it out of your mind. You'll never be able to unsee— unfeel—it."

"I get your point, but what if I live a charmed life from now on, so the worst things that I'm going to live through have already happened—like my break-ups or the death of my grandparents when I was in grade school?" Nora said, contemplatively rolling the stem of her empty wine glass between her thumb and index finger.

"Not to sound maudlin, but since you mentioned grandparents, in actuarial terms your parents are also going to die before you do—that's a given—well, unless you should die an untimely death, which I don't think you'd want to consider either." Sally looked Nora in the eyes. "Do you want to know when and how your parents die? Really think this over; if you still want to make a wish, you should rank your desires and start with the one with the lowest ranking—start with number three. That's what I've decided to do."

"Okay, like, I see your point," said Nora setting her glass back on the table. "What if we meet up again next week after we've each talked with Lucky D? We can go down this rabbit-hole together."

"Ha, maybe we should call it a dragon-hole," Sally said before tipping her glass so sharply that it touched her nose, not willing to waste the last drop of Merlot.

CHAPTER 16 ~ NORA

Nora spent the next week ruminating on the Lucky Dragon's offer, which was far better than ruminating on her canceled wedding. In what order should she take her wishes? Sally had advised starting small with her least valuable wish. *What would it be? Definitely not getting Brad back—that has to be number one. Maybe Melanie's time?* But that felt pretty valuable to Nora, too, especially after Melanie's recent visit. It had reminded her of their inseparable college days. *Maybe time with Melanie should be my second wish?* Suddenly her talk with Dr. Rogers and her failed request for a raise flashed through her head. *Can I wish for a raise? Oh, but it can't be that.* . . She had never been paid more than she was paid at Mill City Physical Therapy right now. . . but maybe she could get the money back that she'd saved for the wedding. Her savings account, which she'd dutifully filled with her paychecks and tips from Gina's for years, had been nearly depleted by wedding expenses. Brad had paid for a few things, sure, but as the bride, most of the bigger expenses—like the venue deposit, flower deposit, catering fee, and that damn dress that she couldn't return—had fallen on her and her parents. *Yes, getting back that money seems like a very good third wish!*

She gave some more thought to Sally's warning. Could something really terrible be lurking in her future, waiting for her? What would it be like to know that something bad was coming? Would it change how she lived her life? For instance, if she were to find out that she was in a bad car accident, would she avoid riding in cars altogether? That seemed impossible; Minneapolis was such a car-centric city. *Even if I give up my Civic, the buses and light rail only go so many places. . .*

She was getting ahead of herself, though. She had no idea what horrors awaited her. As Sally had said, the deaths of her parents were very likely. Despite her somewhat strained relationship with her mom, Deb's death would be incredibly hard to face. But what Nora truly feared was her dad's death. Jim had doted on Nora her whole life, and she'd reciprocated by being a daddy's girl. After her engagement had ended, while her mom seethed over the loss of money, the loss of Nora's relationship with Brad—

and her feelings about it—were what mattered to her father. Her father had been the first person she'd called after leaving the downtown condo that awful day. The two had spent hours on the phone post-breakup.

But, Jim's death had to be the worst thing that was to come for Nora, right? *So, that won't happen until I wish for Brad—*

"Earth to Nora. Did you hear me?" Barb snapped her fingers in front of Nora's face, bringing her back to the Mill City Physical Therapy office. "Where'd you go?"

Barb had been treating Nora with kid gloves since finding out the wedding had been canceled, so this curtness was actually a nice change.

"Oh, um, nowhere. Just spacing out," Nora said. She reached out for the file that Barb had been trying to hand her.

Barb seemed to soften again, back to the nurturing, maternal figure she'd been during the past weeks. "I understand, sweetie. It's been a hard time for you. I know," she said. "I hope you have something nice planned for the weekend."

Nora smiled at the thought of having a once-again full bank account. "I think I do."

~

The Lucky Dragon's white brick walls gleamed in the low-angled light; the slight coating of autumn snow made it almost blinding to walk toward the building. Nora, squinting as she reached the door, saw the OPEN sign in the window.

She walked into the cozy bookshop and knocked the snow from her boots onto the rug. The shop looked much the way it had during Nora's first visit, right down to the cheery fire in the fireplace and coffee mug. This time, black and white cookies that looked like they were from her favorite New York City deli were sitting by the armchair. The cat that had been in the chair during her first visit came up to greet her and rubbed its body along her shin before Nora stooped down to pet it.

"It's good to see you again, Nora," the Lucky Dragon said.

Nora stood after having scratched the kitty behind its ears. "I've made my decision, LD," Nora said, using one of the nicknames that Sally had given the spectral voice.

"No pleasantries? You don't want a cookie and some coffee? Maybe peruse the shelves?" the dragon sighed. "Why do I even put so much work into this place? All you seem to care about is that cat."

Nora, nervous and anxious to leave, ignored his questions. "I'd like to have my savings back. The money that I spent on the wedding, I want it all back," she said.

"Do you agree to the terms of this wish? A vision of one of your worst experiences yet to come in exchange for refilling your coffers?" LD asked.

"I do," Nora said, her hands clutched in front of her coat as though in prayer.

"Alright, it's done. But don't tell me I didn't warn you," said the dragon.

Nora pulled her phone from her pocket, signed into her online banking app, and gasped. Sure enough, her savings account now showed a deposit of over $11,000, made only moments earlier.

"Did you not believe me?" LD asked, sounding a little hurt by Nora's skepticism.

"You have to understand how strange it is to have a wish granted. This is like something out of a fairy tale," Nora said, still staring at her phone's screen.

"It may be from a fairy tale, but this isn't the Disney kind," said the dragon.

Nora looked up from her phone. "What's that supposed to mean?"

The Lucky Dragon chuckled. "Ever read the originals? Brothers Grimm? Hans Christian Andersen?"

"Yes. . . ohhh," Nora said, recalling the grisly details of stepsisters cutting off toes and heels to fit in the glass slipper.

"It's a bit like that."

Nora shuddered, wondering if she'd made a terrible mistake as she turned to leave.

~

"Mom? Dad? I'm here," Nora said, opening the front door of her parent's suburban split level using her key. She hadn't lived in the house since she was eighteen, except very briefly after moving back from New York, but it still felt like home.

"In here, sweetheart," called her dad from the kitchen.

Jim was at the stove, wearing an apron that read "WORLD'S OKAYEST COOK," which had been a Christmas gift from Nora when she was in high school. She walked over and kissed him on the cheek as he stirred chicken noodle soup in the big pot that had served as Nora's first bathtub after she'd come home from the hospital. She'd been such a tiny baby that the new parents were afraid she might slip from their hands if they tried to wash her in the full-size tub. She didn't remember this, of course, but there was a photo of her being bathed in the kettle hanging on the wall in her parents' guest bathroom.

"You're just in time for dinner. Are you hungry?" Jim asked, while grinding some pepper into the soup.

"Famished. Thanks, Dad. Is Mom around?" Nora opened the fridge and dug around for one of Deb's Diet Cokes.

Jim blew on a spoonful of hot soup. "I think she's down in the laundry room. Can you tell her that food'll be ready in five minutes?" he asked before tasting his creation.

"Will do," Nora said. She cracked open the can of soda on her way to the basement.

"Mom, are you down here?" Nora called as she descended the stairs. The semi-finished basement had both frightened her as a child and been a refuge in her teen years. The summer before she started high school, she'd put a beanbag chair and floor lamp in the large lower room so she could read in its subterranean coolness on hot summer days.

"In here, Nora," her mother replied.

Nora went into the laundry room, pulled a piece of paper from her pocket, and handed it to her mom.

"What's this?" Deb said, taking the check and unfolding it.

"It's everything I owe you and Dad for the wedding."

"How did you get this?" Deb gaped at her, then looked back down at the check.

"Let's just say I came into some money," Nora said.

Deb's eyes got big. "Did you do something illegal? No, don't tell me—I don't want to know."

"I didn't do anything illegal, Mom." Nora chuckled. "You just wouldn't believe me if I told you how I came by it."

"Well, hmm, okay then. Thank you. This is very responsible of you. It means a lot," Deb said, still clutching the check with both boney hands.

"You're welcome. Let's go tell Dad and eat—it looked like his soup is ready."

Following her mother up the stairs, Nora smiled what might have been her first genuine smile in a week. "Thanks, LD," she whispered to the ether. She assumed he heard when the stairwell lightbulb above her head flickered, and she caught a whiff of what smelled like cigar smoke instead of chicken soup.

The painful weight in Nora's chest felt like a stone. No, a boulder. But it wasn't physical. It was emotional pain from sitting at her father's bedside, watching him slip away.

The cancer had spread to several organs by the time anyone knew that it was happening. The doctors said that had they caught it earlier, Jim's chances would have been good, but with the late diagnosis, there wasn't anything the medical team could do except make him comfortable as he reached the end. Palliative care, they called it.

It had seemed like it had been "the end" for the last full week. Nora had barely left her father's bedside. She held his hand, but with all the weight he'd lost, it felt fragile—

not like the big, strong hands that had made Nora feel so protected as a child.

Jim opened his eyes and met Nora's gaze, his eyes hazy with pain.

"Sweetie," he croaked, his voice barely above a whisper.

"I'm here, Dad," Nora said, holding back tears again. She didn't want him to see her cry. It would only distress him.

"There's something I need to tell you. You need to know—" his words cut off by a dry cough. Nora picked up the glass from the table beside the bed and helped Jim take a sip of water.

"It's okay, Dad. I know you love me," she said, putting the glass back on the table.

"It's. . . we always meant to tell you. It just. . . it never felt like the right time," he said, squeezing Nora's hand with what must have been the last of his strength.

"What is it?" she said, fear fluttering in her chest at her father's words.

"Your mom and I, we couldn't conceive. We tried everything and it just never worked for us," he said.

"I know. I was your miracle baby."

"Nora, you were a miracle, but you're not ours. Your mother, your biological mother, passed away after giving birth to you," he said, tears coming down his face.

"What?" Nora said, the world seeming to bend with this revelation.

"Sweetie, you're my daughter and I chose you and I love you," he said. "But you deserve to know that you might have other family out there, and I think you should try to find them after I'm gone. You deserve to know the truth about who you are." At that, Jim closed his eyes, brought Nora's hand to his heart, and slipped back into morphine-induced sleep.

Nora knew that was the last time he'd wake up. She rested her head on his chest and finally let herself weep.

CHAPTER 17 ~ SALLY

Sally walked into the kitchen, tossed her purse on the counter, and rushed to the living room still in her coat. Just back from her latest visit with the Lucky Dragon, she was in a hurry to see if he had fulfilled her wish. It was crazy and she was crazy for believing that it could come true, but now that she'd wished it, she could think of nothing else.

Sally lifted the fallboard covering the keys and sat down at the piano. She adjusted her position and then, using both hands, ran through chromatic scales up and down the keyboard. Sally raised her hands, palms toward her face, and shook her head in open-mouthed amazement. She flexed her hands—they had known what to do. The holy brain-to-hand connection contained within every good instrumentalist was hers once again. She closed her eyes and thought about music. After so many years of piano competitions, she'd had a huge number of difficult pieces committed to memory. She had been perfecting Liszt's *La Campanella* before the accident; could she play it? She placed her hands at the right end of the keyboard and began. Notes cascaded from the instrument in rapid succession. Sally's hands came down on the final chord with the same control that she'd maintained throughout the nearly impossible piece. She lifted her hands from the keyboard and dropped them to her lap as tears filled her eyes. Oh, how she had missed this. Other than her parents, the piano had been her first love, and now she had it back. *After so many years of lying to myself that it didn't matter, I have it back. I really have it back! Hallelujah!*

Music filled the house for the next hour, however Sally was careful to quit playing before Tiffany arrived home. She couldn't explain her regained prowess in any manner that didn't make her sound as though she'd lost her mind. There was no explanation, but if this was losing her mind, she was willing to bid her wits both *sayonara* and *arrivederci*. The only repercussion, other than the joy that she was experiencing, was the ache in her right shoulder, arms, wrists, and fingers. Her body was out of shape for the rigors of the keyboard. Sally figured the pains would pass with practice, which she understood she would have to maintain if she were to keep and grow her skills; Lucky D had told her as much. Besides, she'd already decided that her next wish would be for her body to be physically the best it had ever been—she would have her playing muscles back.

~

"Thanks for making my favorite hot dish for supper," Tiffany said as she carried the remains of the sausage and penne concoction to the kitchen counter.

"My pleasure, sweetie. I'm going to try to make all your favorites before you leave. I want to you to remember all the reasons you should come home from Spain."

"Don't be silly, Mom—I'm sure to come home. I'll miss you guys and your money."

"Oh, you are such a kind and thoughtful daughter," Sally said as she snapped the dishtowel at Tiffany.

Tiffany dodged the towel. "Duh—you and Daddy raised me right."

"I know you were kidding, but I really hope we did. I never expected that you'd be leaving me by myself so soon—this is a big step for you."

"Yeah, I really appreciate you and Dad letting me do this. But, Mom, you're hardly being left alone. I mean, I know Trudy's moving, but it's not like Daddy's going anywhere."

"I suppose. . . It's just not going to be the same," said Sally as thousands of thoughts swirled in her head. "I keep wondering if this will be our last Thanksgiving under one roof."

"What do you mean, Mom?"

Sally paused, then said, "Trudy doesn't know where Enrique will find a position—with his specialty it could be anywhere in the world. They might not be able to get back every year."

"You worry too much." Tiffany motioned toward a stool at the kitchen counter. "Come here." As soon as Sally sat down, Tiff put her hands on her mother's shoulders and massaged the tension knots in her neck and back. Sally moaned with pleasure and thought about how sweet her teen daughter could be when the mood hit her, never mind that it usually hit her when she wanted something.

Bruce was snoring by the time Sally went to bed. She'd stayed up late going through the sheet music in the piano bench and checking online to see what she might need to purchase to keep her skills sharp. Neither of her daughters had ever reached her level of proficiency, so most of the newer music in the house was far too basic. She'd found a few of her old exercise books that would be useful for a month or two, but performance pieces she'd have to order. The thought of not playing while Tiffany and Bruce were at home was killing Sally, but she knew that it was too soon for them to hear her. By the time Tiff returned from Spain, Sally's regained abilities might seem plausible. As for an eventual explanation for Bruce, Sally wasn't completely sure she cared, or that he would even be around to notice. She thought once again about her comment to Tiffany that "this might be our last Thanksgiving under one roof." She'd lied—it was Bruce, not Trudy's family, that she'd envisioned missing from the Thanksgiving table.

Sally rolled over on her side and karate chopped her pillow to fold it in half. Having a thicker, firmer head support took some of the ache out of her neck. She knew that sleep would come slowly tonight, besides contending with Bruce's uneven snoring, she hadn't as yet experienced any bad memories in payment for her regained piano prowess. Lucky D had said that the bill would come due shortly after her wish had been granted; Sally figured it was likely to come tonight in her sleep. What would it be? What was the third worst thing to have ever happened to her? She knew what the worst period in her life had been, but what were the second and third worst? Sally assumed one, or both, might be the deaths of her parents. She had taken her father's death hard. He was young, still in his fifties, when he'd been diagnosed with congestive heart failure. Her mother's death was difficult, but Sally was older and so was her mother. And, as her mother had said in her very matter of fact way, "we all have to go sometime—and, at least, we got it in the right order—I'm going before you.

It's as it should be." She'd always been such a stoic. What other kind of person would have assumed you could just replace one daughter with another, or that proper death order could make pain go away? If one of her parents' deaths wasn't what she would relive tonight, what would it be?

The kiss in front of The Saint Paul Hotel drifted through Sally's mind. No, she didn't want to relive those feelings, but, strangely, she didn't think that Bruce's affair could be the third worst thing that she had ever experienced. It happened—sure—but Bruce was still in bed beside her, snoring away. She had cried and felt betrayed. She still felt betrayed, but in the last few days, she'd been feeling far more anger than sadness. She'd been momentarily devastated, if that were such a thing, but her life had not changed, at least not yet. Sally pushed herself up on her elbow so that she could see over the rumbling lump made by Bruce's prone body. The bedside clock read 1:27 a.m.—she really should fall asleep. . .

The pain. It was all she could feel at first. Everything HURT! She tried to cry out.

Where am I? Am I still in the car?

Where's Ben? Ben. . . Ben. . . Benny!

Help me, please, please help me!

Sally couldn't move. She felt tied down by her throat—there was something around her neck. She began to lift her hand; someone held it down and said, "Try not to move, Sally. You can't talk—you're intubated. There's a tube down your throat."

The pain, stabbing, shooting, all-encompassing agony was all she felt. Sally's body began to quake.

"We're going to give you something to quiet you," came the calming voice.

Wait, where's Ben? Our baby, where's. . .

Sally awakened hours later. *It's still dark—no that's not it—my eyes are shut. I can't open them. Are they taped closed? Could they be?* The weight still pressed against her neck and the pains in her lower torso felt like she was being stabbed repeatedly by a hundred serrated knives. Her legs, especially her left, felt as though on fire.

I must be in the hospital. What happened? She tried to reach toward her abdomen, but someone stopped her. That voice again, "It's okay; your babies are okay—tiny, but healthy."

The baby. I had my baby. My baby's fine. My baby's okay. . . Where's Ben? Sally didn't reach out but slapped her palm on the hard ICU bed. The calming voice returned, "You were in a car accident. Do you remember? You are hurt, but your babies are fine. The boy you were with was hurt—he's not here. He's been flown to Rochester. You both have head injuries. . ."

Ben was hurt. Oh, Benny. . . I'm so cold, I'm so cold. . . hold me Ben. . . hold me. . . Sally began to shake violently. An alarm sounded.

"She's having another seizure. We're going to have to do something more for her or she's not going to make it through the ni. . ." The voices faded as Sally drifted into unconsciousness.

~

Sally opened her eyes and stirred. Bruce looked at her from beside the closet door. "That musta been one hell of a dream you had last night."

"Yeah, good morning to you, too." Sally said, finishing the greeting in her head with an unspoken *dickhead.*

"No, really, Sal, I coulda sworn you were having a seizure the way you were grunting and rolling around."

"It wasn't good, but I'm okay now," Sally said, pulling the blankets up to her chin in the chilly bedroom.

"—I was kinda worried."

"But not enough to wake me? Thanks for your concern. . ." *Asshole.*

Bruce shrugged and walked into the closet continuing to dress for his day at the office. Sally rolled over, her face toward the wall, and thought about what she'd experienced. It had not been a dream. She had just relived the third worst event of her life to date. She didn't disbelieve that it had happened to her, but she hadn't remembered any of it before last night. The physical pain she'd experienced was unfathomable. It made the horrible pains she remembered from those early years seem like minor headaches and compared to the normal aches she was feeling this morning—well, next to the pains she'd experienced right after the accident—they were like pin pricks.

Sally tried to remember the nurse's words: "The babies are fine."—*No that can't be right—the baby's fine. The baby's okay. That had to have been what she'd said.* Sally's memories drifted to tiny Trudy—she was indeed fine; the nurse was right. But Ben? Sally didn't remember anything about him being in Rochester. When she'd come to, months after she had been put into a drug-induced coma, Ben was gone. She'd always assumed he'd died in the accident. No one had wanted to talk about it—not even Ben's mother, who, according to Sally's folks, blamed Sally for her son's death. Her mother told Sally that Mrs. Bradley had left the area with Ben's ashes and asked to be left alone. That was Sally's worst day—the day she found out that Ben had died. That was the day she feared reliving. Tears dampened the pillow that she hugged to her face while she sobbed.

~

"Thanks for having me over, Nora," Sally said as she handed Nora her coat.

"No problem, thanks for coming." Nora placed Sally's coat over the back of a modern black-pleather couch.

"Nice couch," Sally said.

"Thanks—I got it for fifty bucks off Craigslist."

Sally continued to look around the room. She thought the couch an odd piece for Nora to have mixed with the other furniture in the old studio apartment, but it seemed to work with the bright and eclectic mix of antiques, and what Sally could only assume were family—or street curb—castoffs.

"Would you like to sit at the table? I've made coffee—or you could have tea if you prefer. . . but, I don't have a big selection," Nora said somewhat apologetically.

"Coffee's fine. I like both—give me caffeine in almost any form and I'm happy."

"And awake, I'd imagine," Nora said, pouring a cup from her Mr. Coffee carafe.

"It does help," replied Sally, once again looking around Nora's apartment. "Your place is really cute, yet, somehow, sophisticated. Those two adjectives don't sound like they go together, but in this case they do. Truth is, your place looks like you." Sally couldn't help but remember the first time she had seen Nora in the Lucky Dragon parking lot. She still thought she could see some of Trudy's features in Nora's face, but she now realized it was more the way the two women held their bodies and moved through space that made them resemble one another.

"Aww, thanks Sally." Nora carried the coffees from the tiny kitchen counter to a high glass-topped table and set them down next to a footed plate of store-bought cookies.

"Thank you," said Sally, "So, I assume we're going to recap how our first wishes went, right?"

"First wishes and first payments—if you're willing to share that information." Nora blew on her coffee and looked at Sally expectantly.

Sally told Nora about how she'd wished to regain her skills at the piano. "I was in a bad accident when I was young—in my teens. That's how I lost my ability to play piano—I lost my ability to do most everything. Relearning to talk and walk again took precedence over music."

"So, what was the payment? Was it horrible?" Nora asked.

"Yes and no. It had to do with that accident, too. I've never remembered the details from when I first woke up from my injuries. Well, not until LD brought them to me in my dreams. Not dreams, really; more like reliving—coming back to life shortly after the crash. The physical pain was unbelievably intense, and much of what I heard—I couldn't see anything—didn't make sense. It's still all very confusing. But, LD was true to his word. I can play the piano again. It's truly a miracle."

Nora pushed the plate of cookies toward Sally and asked, "Do you think it's worth asking for more wishes to be granted?"

"Yeah, at least one. I'm just not sure that I'll ask for my top wish—unlike you, I know what my payment will be. I don't think I'm willing to go there no matter what the prize. What about you?" Sally bit into a cookie; part of it crumbled and fell back to the glass top of the table. She absentmindedly brushed the crumbs into a pile as she concentrated on Nora's words.

"Oh, I was crass and wished for money—I asked for my savings account to be as big as it had ever been—as big as it had been before paying for all the stuff for a wedding that didn't happen."

"Did you get it?"

"Got it and already spent part of it. I paid my parents back—which felt great. The problem came with my payment to LD."

"Oh, that's right," Sally grimaced, "a future tragedy—what did you learn?"

"I learned that you were right. . . I had to pre-experience my father's death and his really strange deathbed confession to me. I can't get it out of my head; his death was so horrible and the confession, well. . . I need someone to talk to about all this."

"What did he tell you?"

"Right before he died, he told me that I'm adopted. I know that can't be true—he must have been hallucinating from the drugs. . . but, what really bothered me was seeing him dying from cancer—it was awful. I'm not sure I'll ever be able to look at him again and not see him looking like he did in that bed."

"Oh, Nora, I'm so sorry—but maybe you can try to think of him as having been ill and gotten better."

"But that's not what's going to happen," said Nora as she twisted the paper napkin she'd been holding into a knot.

"Are you sure? Didn't the dragon say that if you stay on the same course in life these are the things that will happen?"

"Yes, but—"

"But what if you can get him to discover his cancer earlier? Sometimes that makes all the difference in outcomes."

"How am I going to do that? I don't know when in the future this happened. . . happens. I don't even know what kind of cancer he had, or—I guess I mean—gets. And all that crazy stuff about adoption—where'd that come from? Was that the drugs talking—it had to be, right?"

"Maybe. . . But, as far as the cancer goes, can you encourage him to get yearly checkups? Maybe you can find some knowledgeable party to talk to about all of this. . .

even discussing it with a close friend—someone who knows your dad. . .”

Nora stared glumly out the multi-paned window beside the table and rolled the tattered paper napkin between her palms. “Finding someone to talk to was—is—going to be my second wish. I’ve been planning on wishing for more time with my friend Melanie. I really miss her.”

“A good friend to lean on would help. What happened? Did she move away?” Sally asked.

“No, but she got married and had a baby—we just don’t seem to get together like we used to,” Nora said.

“I understand longing for your old friend, but I’d be careful with that wish.”

“Why? I really need her now.”

“You still have her friendship, but think about why you aren’t spending time with her. . . If something bad happened to her husband or child, she’d possibly have more time for you, but at what cost to her?”

“You don’t know that that’s how it would work,” Nora said defensively.

“No, but are you willing to risk your friend’s happiness for your own? Maybe there are good reasons why you shouldn’t make any more wishes.”

“Yeah, I get that—but it seems like I’d be throwing away two fantastic opportunities to change my life for the better. I mean not many people get this kind of magic handed to them.”

"I know, but just. . . just promise me that you'll think about it. As LD says, we should be careful what we wish for. Please be sure, Nora."

CHAPTER 18 ~ NORA

On Saturday morning, Nora stood outside the white brick and black shuttered building that no longer looked anything like a Chinese restaurant. Instead, it looked like the "after shot" of a structure from one of those HGTV shows where the snarky, beautiful wife and the golden retriever-like husband flip derelict buildings.

"Nora! Hey!" said a familiar voice.

Nora let her hand drop from the door handle of the Lucky Dragon, turning toward the person who had greeted her by name. "Oh, hi, D'Wight! What are you doing here? Wait, do you visit the dragon, too?"

"Huh? Oh, the building. I still live upstairs, remember?"

"Right, I forgot." Nora shook her head.

"So, were you on your way somewhere?"

"I. . . ah. . . was just in the neighborhood and thought I'd stop by to see what was happening to your building," Nora replied, nearly choking on the lie.

"Not my building and not much progress, as you can see," D'Wight replied as he gestured toward the magnificent white exterior.

"Well, I suppose I should go so that you can be on your way," Nora said, realizing again that D'Wight saw none of the changes to the building that had charmed her so completely.

"I am actually on my way to this really cool event at the Minnesota Center for Book Arts. You wouldn't want to maybe join me, would you?" he said, ducking his head and rubbing the back of his neck.

Nora paused, thinking about her visit to the Lucky Dragon and her wish. She'd spent all morning going back and forth about asking for another wish. Her talk with Sally, even though she had dismissed it at the time, had made her reassess asking for more of Melanie's attention— she didn't want to risk upsetting her best friend's life. But her biggest wish—having Brad back so her life could start—was still on the table. Funny thing was, now that she'd run into D'Wight, even her biggest wish didn't seem all that important. . .

"What's the event?" asked Nora.

"Oh, it's an exhibit by this artist who does sculptures with books. Don't worry, none of the books are damaged," he added quickly, having seen Nora cringe at the thought of cutting up books. "I thought it might give me some ideas for my installations. I've been trying to think of how I could bring my art to the next level, and I've always found that looking at what others are doing helps spark my creativity. So. . . will you come with me?"

"Yeah, that sounds really cool. I'd love to see you in your element again." Nora remembered seeing D'Wight in the Lucky Dragon parking lot with his arms around the raven-haired woman and decided she had no reason to think of this impromptu outing as a date and continued, "I mean, around art."

"Awesome. I can drive us over there if you don't mind leaving your car. I promise not to tow it." D'Wight grinned and gestured to Nora's Honda, once again parked in the Lucky Dragon parking lot.

"That'd be great. Thanks. I hope the new owners feel the same way," Nora said and smiled back with what she hoped was a platonic grin.

~

A few hours later, Nora was seated in the armchair next to the fireplace in the Lucky Dragon's bookshop. Nora and D'Wight had gone to see the book sculpture exhibit and then stopped for a coffee and muffin in the adjoining coffee shop. The art was fantastic, but the conversation was even better: they talked about D'Wight's art, about Nora's lifelong love of books, about the dreams they'd had as kids. They talked about their families. D'Wight had lost his parents, but had sisters who still lived in the area, and he adored his nieces and nephews. Nora talked about what it was like to be an only child and some of the pressures that came along with that. Things got deep at times, but they laughed a lot. In fact, Nora couldn't remember the last time she'd laughed so much. Or the last time she'd gone so long without thinking about Brad. Well, truthfully, she had thought about Brad once while looking at the art exhibit, but only to ponder how much he would have hated it.

The cat leapt up on the arm of the chair, bringing Nora out of her reflection. She scratched the purring cat under the chin.

"Well, Nora, how was your first wish and payment?" asked the voice of the Lucky Dragon.

"Good. . . confusing, but good," Nora said, picking up the coffee that had just the right amount of cream and taking a sip.

"Oh? Why do you say that?" Lucky D asked.

"Well, the money was great. I was able to pay back my parents for their help with the wedding expenses and still have some left over."

"That's good. I'm always pleased when a wish I grant is useful."

"But, I still don't understand my payment," she said.

"How is that?" Lucky D inquired.

"Well, when I went to sleep after our last meeting, I had a vivid dream about my dad's death. It did feel terrible, but I guess I can't tell if it was real or not. Was that my payment?"

"Indeed, it was your payment, and it was also very real. That might not be what happens in the end, but it was both of your destinies at that moment in time."

"But, I think my dad told me that I'm. . . not his actual daughter?—that I'm adopted. But that's insane. I look like them. . . well, I thought I looked like them. Maybe I've been seeing what I want to see. But how could they have lied to me for so long? I'm thirty-five-years-old, for God's sake!"

"Well, don't you think that could be one of the reasons it's a bad moment? Finding out deathbed secrets is never good for those left behind. They are confusing and often inaccurate—those confessions only help alleviate the conscience of those doing the leaving."

"I suppose that's true, but if that was my third worst payment, I'm not excited to find out what the top two are," said Nora. "Wait—you said that the payment was only what my life *could* look like—not what it *will* look like, right?"

"Yes, Nora. You decide your own destiny. You make your own luck," said the dragon. "Now, have you decided on your next wish?"

"I. . ." Nora opened her mouth, preparing to declare that she was ready for her biggest wish—for Brad to love her as much as he did when he'd asked her to marry him over a year ago. But she paused, realizing that this morning with D'Wight had been one of her best mornings in a long time—a really, really long time. Even when they were deeply in love, she didn't think Brad would have enjoyed the book sculpture exhibit. In fact, after their first year of dating, she and Brad had rarely done things together that were her choice.

"Yes?" asked the dragon with a hint of a smile in his voice.

"I don't think I'm ready. I thought I was, but. . ."

"But?"

"I'm just not ready," Nora said, rising from the armchair. The cat, disrupted by Nora's sudden movement, jumped down and marched away, tail held high, whiskers in the air.

"Take your time. Wishes are not meant to be taken lightly," LD said as Nora walked toward the door. "Just return when you know what you want."

Nora paused at the door and turned around to look at the bookshop with its perfect cozy reading nooks and curated selection of her favorite novels. It really was the bookshop of her dreams. Just the kind of place she would love to work.

"I'll do that," Nora said as she reached the door that magically swung open to let her out into the chilly fall air.

CHAPTER 19 ~ SALLY

Early in the week before Thanksgiving, Sally returned to the Lucky Dragon building. It looked just as it had when she'd visited in previous weeks; it was still a lovely shade of dusty lilac with implausible purple blooms filling its window boxes. Sally parked in the empty lot beside the building and gingerly shuffled her feet through the light snow covering the blacktop. She thought about how Thanksgiving was supposed to be a harvest festival—in this part of the country, it seemed about a month too late for piles of ripe produce and bouquets of autumn leaves. As Sally approached the building's front door, it swung open.

"Welcome, welcome, welcome," came Lucky D's mirthful growl. "You're back—I didn't frighten you away?"

"Not yet," Sally said.

"Sit—your tea is ready."

"You were expecting me?"

"Well, yes, I always know when company is on the horizon."

Sally had slipped off her coat and hung it on the back of the delicate gold chair. She took a drink from the steaming cup in front of her. "This is delicious. So delicate, yet smokey. What's it called?"

"Keemun," the dragon replied. "I don't enjoy it as much as I do Lapsang Souchong, which I've heard called 'Dragon's breath,' but I assumed Keemun's delicate flavor would be more your *cup o' tea.*"

"Bad pun—but true. It's like it's almost smoky—malty maybe."

"Are you here to make a wish or discuss tea? I'll do either with you, but I would imagine you're more interested in wishes. Speaking of which, how are your piano skills?"

"It's wonderful to be able to play again. I guess that's why I'm back for a second go-round with the wishes. I'd like to have my body feel as good as it did when I was seventeen. I wanted to be pain free before you returned my ability to play the piano, but now I want good health so that I have the physical stamina to play up to my potential."

"So, health is what we're talking about? You'd like to be as healthy as you have ever been?"

"Yes, healthy and pain free. I assume those two things go together?"

"Generally, and I'm quite sure that will be the case for you," Lucky D said.

"Then, that's my second wish."

"Granted. Please, finish your tea before you leave. I'll sit here and wait."

Sally took another drink of the clear, coppery-red brew and looked around the elegant room. Just like the other times that she had visited, a fire burned in the brick fireplace situated on the far wall. A small calico cat was curled up on the back of one of the velvet couches. "Has the kitty always been here? I've never noticed it before."

"Yes," replied the dragon. "She's always lived here. She had to live upstairs when this building was a restaurant—health codes, you know—but rules are a bit laxer in magical teashops. Speaking of lax rules, mind if I smoke?"

"I do—but I don't want to seem ungrateful. Light up; I'm almost done with my tea." Sally heard a match being pulled across a striker, followed by the sound of puffing. The smell of cigar smoke began to fill the room. "I'll take that as my cue to leave," Sally said taking the last swallow of her tea.

As Sally stood, she knocked over the chair where she'd been sitting. "Whew, standing happened with a bit more vigor than I'd expected—please excuse my clumsiness." She lifted her coat from off the floor, noticing that she had no problems bending over, and, when she slipped her arm though the peacoat's satin-lined sleeve, there was no pain in her right shoulder. Sally walked toward the door that swung open as she neared. "Thank you, LD—I feel great!"

"Goodbye, Sally. I hope you continue to be pleased with the deal we just made."

Sally nearly bounded toward her SUV. No more shuffling through the snow for her. Her footing was sure, and she figured that her bones were as strong as they'd been when she was a child—if she fell, she'd bounce!

~

Sally was baffled by her continual need to collect recipes for different versions of green bean casserole and sausage dressing considering she never made anything other than the dishes she'd grown up with. Magazine and newspaper clippings littered the floor after falling from the manilla folder labeled "Thanksgiving" that she'd carelessly pulled from the top shelf of the kitchen cabinet above the fridge. Sally giggled as she dropped to the floor to pick up the scraps of paper. "I FEEL SO GOOD!!!" she shouted to the empty house, before crossing her legs and standing with the bulging folder clutched to her chest. "Look, Ma, no hands!" she shouted, just as Tiffany walked into the kitchen.

"What, Mom? Are you okay?"

"Oh, sorry, honey—I was just talking to myself. Everything's fine—more than fine. I feel great. I'm just starting to get ready for Thanksgiving."

"Oh, that reminds me—about Thanksgiving—"

"Don't tell me—"

"Mom, jeez, let me finish. I just wanna know what time we're eating."

"Sorry. We're eating early this year, probably around noon."

"That is early—why?" Tiffany asked as she opened the refrigerator and rummaged through the contents before selecting a yogurt and tearing off the foil lid with her teeth.

"Your dad's request. Seems he needs to be in Duluth by early evening to help get ready for some Black Friday promotion that he's cooked-up. I already talked to Trudy—she seemed happy about it—thinks an early dinner will work better for the boys."

"Okay—I promised Amanda I'd come over a few times before I leave for Barcelona. I'll let her know if I visit on Thanksgiving it'll have to be afternoon or evening." Tiffany grabbed a spoon from the drawer, a granola bar from the counter, and headed toward the stairs. "Is Daddy home?"

"No, he had to work late tonight. Anything I can help with?"

"Nah, just need to ask him something—it's like I never see him anymore."

"Yeah, he keeps himself busy," said Sally, hoping she didn't sound too disgusted.

~

Sally pulled the sheet and blanket to her chin. What a gift it was to crawl into bed and not ache anywhere. She wondered if her newly granted good health would allow her to fall asleep as quickly as she had when she was a teenager—that would be a bonus. Bruce still wasn't home, so at least she didn't have to contend with his snoring while she waited for the sandman. . .

Sally knocked at the hospice room door. When she didn't hear anything but her father's labored breathing, she walked into the room, removed her coat, and hung it on a peg by the door. The room was meant to look like a cozy bedroom, but with a bulletin board hung beneath a wall-mounted TV, it looked like a hospital room attempting to disguise itself with polyester lace curtains and framed prints of baskets of puppies. Sally thought if her dad were lucid, not actively dying, he would have commented on being surrounded by such sappy decor. Sally pulled a padded chair over to her father's bedside, sat, and gently lifted his hand. "Daddy, I'm here. A nurse phoned and said that you wanted to talk with me tonight."

Sally's father stirred slightly, but didn't open his eyes.

"Trudy made you a card. She wanted me to bring it, but I said that I'd let her bring it to you when we all come visit tomorrow." Sally squeezed her father's hand, and he lightly squeezed her hand in response, then he slowly opened his eyes. An almost visible closed-mouth smile crossed his lips when he saw his only daughter's face. "Hi, Daddy," was all Sally could muster when she looked into his half-closed eyes. A tear ran down her cheek.

"I'm sorry, honey. . ." he said in a slow, quiet rasp, his voice weak because he lacked the lung power needed for speech.

"Oh, Daddy, I am too. You shouldn't have to go through this."

"No. . . no, you don't understand."

"What, Daddy?"

"We. . . your mother and I shouldn't have done it."

"Oh, please, if you're talking about fighting with me over Trudy, don't worry about it. It's over and done with. I forgave you and Mom a long time ago. Trudy loves you and so do I. Please, please, Daddy—don't feel bad."

"No, the other one. . ."

"Bruce? He's forgiven you, too. It's all okay," Sally said as she squeezed her father's cool limp hand again.

"No, the other, the other one. . ." Sally's father's eyes closed as he drifted into sleep.

Sally gently pushed her father's arm closer to his body and laid her head on the bed beside their clasped hands. She thought of all that her father had done for her over her lifetime, most of it twice: helping her learn to walk, talk, read, and write—helping her learn to ride a bike and drive a car. Everything twice—once before the accident, once after. Her mom had been around, but she'd been busy caring for Trudy; her dad had been Sally's rock. She'd known for years that he'd regretted his part in the custody battle for Trudy. That he felt he still needed to apologize made Sally sad. She would come tomorrow with Bruce and Trudy, and her dad would see that all was forgiven. . .

Sally awoke with her father's hand in hers. He was still. Too still. Sally stood and laid her ear to his chest. She couldn't hear a heartbeat and ran to the nurses' desk for help. "My father, he's not breathing—I think he's—"

"It's okay, Sally," the hospice nurse said as she came from behind the counter and guided Sally back to her father's room. Sally stood by the door as the nurse lifted Sally's father's hand, and then held her stethoscope to his chest and looked at her watch. "Your father has passed, Sally. We'll need to contact your mother. Would you like to make the call, or should we?"

"Could you? I don't know how to tell her."

"Certainly. You can wait here with your father if you'd like or come out to the common room. Either's fine—there's no right or wrong."

"I'd like to stay here." By that time, Sally was in tears, and when the nurse left the room, she began to weep in earnest. Sally sat down by her father's bed, her heart full of regret. There was so much she hadn't said to her father. Yes, she'd known he was dying, but no one had expected him to go so quickly. The doctors had said it could be weeks. Sally put her hand on her father's shoulder. "Daddy. . ." was all she could say.

Twenty minutes later, when Sally's mother arrived, Sally was still in the chair by her father's side. Sally stood to greet her mom.

"Why didn't you call me?" were the first words from her mother's mouth.

"I'm sorry—"

"You're always sorry," Sally's mother muttered.

"Mom, the nurse said that she would call."

"No—why didn't you call me before he died? I should have been here—not you." Sally's mother didn't touch her but walked to her husband's bedside.

"I didn't know he was going to die today. He asked me to come see him."

"Why? What did he tell you—he was delirious, you know. Who's to say what he could have said—you can't believe any of it."

"Mommy, he didn't say anything except that he was sorry."

"For what—what did he say he was sorry for?"

"I'm not sure. I think for fighting for custody, but I don't know."

Hearing those words, Sally's mother seemed to calm. Her focus redirected toward her dead husband and away from making her already distraught daughter feel even worse.

As the days dragged on with the minutia of making arrangements for the funeral and notifying family and friends, Sally's mother's harsh words faded. Sally told herself that her mother was upset and was feeling guilty for not having been by her husband's side when he'd died. Sally told herself that guilt and anger were part of grieving—she'd learned that while still in her teens. She had to forgive her mother; she was the only parent Sally had left. . .

~

Sally stared at the ceiling. Tears ran from the outer corners of her eyes, over her ears, and onto her pillow. *Daddy just died,* thought Sally, before realizing that her father had died when Trudy was barely a teen, decades earlier. *It was a bad dream—ahh, no, it was payment for my wish.*

Bruce had come home at some point in the early morning and was asleep on his side of the bed. Sally looked over his body toward the radio alarm—6:05 a.m., 11-19-18, glowed the red digits on the black plastic screen. The dream had seemed to last for days, and yet only a night had passed. Sally thought of the lines in *A Christmas Carol* when Ebenezer Scrooge said to himself: "The Spirits have done it all in one night. They can do anything they like. Of course they can. Of course they can." Lucky D did it all in one night—*of course he did,* thought Sally.

It was earlier than she usually got up, but Sally left the still-snoring Bruce and walked to their ensuite bathroom. She looked in the mirror as she dried her eyes with a tissue. It was then that she saw the whiteness of her eyes and brightness of her skin and realized, despite her sadness, how good she felt. Nothing hurt—*not a thing!* She thought again of the Dickens' classic and of old Scrooge leaping into the air, shouting for joy. This must have been how he'd felt. He'd gone through a night of hell and he was still in the same old body, but somehow, thanks to something he didn't quite trust or believe in, he was alive once more. Renewed—Scrooge felt renewed. Today, Sally knew just how that felt.

~

"Move to your right, Bruce. Trudy, can you get Ricco to look up? —Good, that's better." Enrique pushed the button on his expensive digital camera sitting atop its tripod and joined the back row of the family grouping. The camera clicked three times in succession before Enrique said, "Just one more time."

"No!" came Bruce's emphatic response. "No more photos—I've got to get on the road."

"Seems the boss has spoken. Bye, fam," Tiffany said as she bounded from the front row toward the stairs heading to her bedroom.

"Thank you for trying, Enrique," Sally said.

"Thanks for asking. This might be the last family photo for. . . well, awhile. I want the boys to remember their Minnesota family just as much as you want them to. I think I got some good shots. I always tend to overdo it."

"I appreciate your effort—I know it's a pain to bring your camera equipment when you have to tote all the boys' things," Sally said.

"Really, it was no problem. You know I'd do anything for you guys after you uprooted your whole lives to move here to be with us when we needed you."

Sally shook her head and gave Enrique a sad smile. "I'm going to miss you all so much. It's not going to be the same around here without you, Trudy, and the boys." She stepped in and hugged her son-in-law.

By mid-afternoon, everyone was gone. Bruce had been the first to leave; he was out the door with his bag by the time Enrique had repacked his camera case. Tiffany flew out the backdoor a few moments after her father. Trudy had offered to stay and help with the dishes, but the boys were getting fussy, and Sally hated to have them miss their afternoon naps. Trudy and Enrique were off to Baltimore on Sunday, and, from what Trudy had said, the couple still had a lot to pack. They needed the unencumbered hours that the boys' naps provided.

Sally stood in the kitchen doorway, her hands on her hips. Thanksgiving was one of those meals that took days to make, minutes to eat, and hours to clean up. And was there any way to fix a Thanksgiving dinner and not have mountains of leftovers? If there was, Sally hadn't found it. She knew she had to pick the meat from the turkey carcass before she cooked the bones for soup, but messing with the sticky meat was one of her least favorite post-turkey tasks. She covered the bird with plastic wrap before heading to the garage fridge—she'd have to face the unpleasant project at some point, but, unlike the dishes, it could wait. On the landing of the steps leading to the garage floor sat Bruce's briefcase. *He must have forgotten it in his hurry to leave,* thought Sally. After making room for the turkey among the cases of beer and pop in the extra fridge, Sally brought the briefcase inside.

She tried to reach Bruce several times on his cell. He didn't pick up, and his phone, for some inexplicable reason, didn't go to voicemail. Knowing it was unlikely that anyone was in the Minneapolis office on Thanksgiving Day, Sally gave Bruce's assistant, Char, a call on her cell. Char didn't answer either, but at least her mailbox wasn't full: "Hi Char, sorry to bother you on Thanksgiving, but Bruce is on his way to Duluth to help out at the new branch, and he forgot his briefcase in our garage. Could you give me a call with that number, or let me know where Bruce is staying so I can call the hotel to find out what he wants me to do? I figure—" Char's phone beeped and the line went dead. *I tried,* thought Sally before returning to the waiting dishes and leftovers.

It took Sally over an hour to clean the kitchen, and, when she'd finally put the last glass in the dishwasher, she rewarded herself by sitting down at the piano. She was engrossed in Chopin when she heard her phone ring in the kitchen. *I'll get it later,* she thought to herself, not willing to take a break from *Opus 9*. She should have been tired after her long day of food prep and clean up, but her once-again healthy body was allowing her to enjoy the long afternoon alone at the piano. When Sally finally checked her phone, there was a message from Char: "Hi Sally, sorry Bruce forgot his briefcase, but you must be confused about what he's doing in Duluth—we have customers there, but we service them out of the Minneapolis office. There's no new Duluth branch. If he's up there, I don't know where he's staying. Sorry. Hope you had a nice Thanksgiving—see you at the Christmas party."

Sally put her phone on the kitchen counter. There was no Duluth branch. His assistant, the woman who knew more about the day-to-day operation of Bruce's business than Bruce did, didn't know where he was. Sally was furious and certain that Bruce didn't need his briefcase to do whatever it was he was doing with his comely redhead. He'd rushed off on Thanksgiving Day, left his family—his daughters, who would both soon be leaving—to spend time with his mistress. Sally wanted to throw something, pummel someone. She went back to the piano and played the opening chords of Carl Orff's *Carmina Burana* with such force that the walls of the living room shook. She played her rage until her arms ached. She had just finished the dramatic piece as Tiffany walked in from the kitchen, surprising her.

"Mom, I didn't know that you could play like that."

"Oh," Sally said, thinking quickly, "I've been practicing while you're at school. Remember, I told you that I used to play pretty well—I thought I'd take it up again since I'm going to have so much time on my hands." Sally felt bad about lying to Tiffany, but then, it wasn't really a lie—she did plan on practicing daily, and it certainly wasn't a lie to say she used to be good. "Did you have a nice time at Amanda's?"

"Yeah, just talked—you know. She's bummed I'm leaving and kinda mad, I think, that she gave up Spain for cheer squad. It's kinda hard to feel sorry for her. I mean, like, she made her decision."

"True, but some decisions are harder to make than others. You know—coulda, woulda, shoulda—the older you get, the more often you have to give up one thing for another," Sally said, thinking of the decision she had just made to kick Bruce out of the house.

"I s'pose," said Tiffany. "I'm not sorry at all for trading winter in Minnesota for winter in Barcelona. It's s'pose to be like sixty degrees in December. . . If you don't need me for anything, I'm gonna start packing my stuff."

"No—I don't need anything. . ." replied the distracted Sally, "I've still got to take the turkey apart, but that's sort of a one-person job. . . Goodnight, hon, if I don't see you before you go to bed."

"'G'night, Mom. Love you."

"Love you, too," *and I'm going to miss you more than you can imagine.*

CHAPTER 20 ~ NORA

"Pick up, Sally. Please, pick up," Nora muttered under her breath. Nora was of the generation that never called a person without an appointment, but she sensed that Sally wouldn't mind, and she needed to talk to someone who wouldn't think she belonged in a psych ward. Nora now realized that Sally had been right, she shouldn't have messed with tragedies of the future. *Tragedies of the Future—* if she weren't so upset by the things that had transpired, Nora would have thought it a great name for an emo band.

Nora heard Sally fumbling with her phone before answering. "Hi, Nora."

"Hi, Sally. Sorry about the call, but I really need to talk to you. Could we meet sometime, or do you have time to talk right now? I really need to get this off my chest."

"Now's fine, or we can meet—whichever."

"Since you have time now, I just wanted to let you know that I'm not going to ask for my other two wishes."

"Okay," Sally responded. "Why did you decide that?"

"The more I thought about it. . . well, this may sound weird, but I don't think I need them. Plus, I definitely don't think they're worth the price of seeing my future tragedies, especially considering that LD or 'the powers that be' thought my dad's death was the least traumatic of the three. It was horrible. What do you think—am I wasting something really special? Do you think I'm wrong?"

"Wrong—no. It's your decision to make. And, if it's any consolation, I agree with you. I've decided to forgo my top wish, too. I *know* my payment's something I'm not willing to revisit, and—this may make me sound flighty—but I don't think the thing I thought I wanted the most is all that important anymore. I've realized that if I'd really wanted it as much as I thought I did, well, I could have done the work and achieved the results on my own. . . I still can—if I really want to," Sally said as she patted her mid-section.

"Sounds familiar—I think I've come to that same realization."

"So, how should we proceed? Do we tell LD or do we just never return to the building?" Sally asked.

"Oh, I think we've got to tell him. And, even though I don't want the wishes, I'd like to see the bookstore one more time. That's a memory I want to keep—I tried taking photos during my last visit, but they vanished as soon as I looked at them."

"Funny—I had the same thing happen. Magic goes poof, I guess. What if we meet up at the building, give LD our news, and then go have coffee somewhere nearby? I'll have to make it quick—it's a busy weekend for my family. What works for you?"

Nora checked the calendar on her phone. "How about Saturday morning? Around 9:00? I work the lunch shift at Gina's this weekend, so quick is good for me too."

"It's a date: 9:00, this Saturday, in front of the Lucky Dragon. Coffee place TBD," Sally said.

Nora parked her Civic in the parking lot of the Lucky Dragon building. It was a few minutes before 9:00. Sally hadn't arrived yet, but that was what Nora had been hoping for. She wanted time to commit the Lucky Dragon building to memory since she assumed it wouldn't look the same after she gave up her final wishes. Nora walked from her car to the front of the old restaurant. It was so perfect: white paint covered the bricks, the trim around the windows and the shutters were high-gloss black and painted with care, the ferns in the window boxes had even been accessorized with twinkle lights, red berries, and gilded pinecones for the season, and the windows above the ferns were so clean that they sparkled in the morning sunlight.

Not ready to go into the building before talking to Sally, Nora pressed her nose against the window of the front door. Through the glass, she saw the perfect bookstore— the store of her dreams. If only she could work at a place like that. Helping customers, choosing books, ordering stock. . . *Even dusting the shelves in a shop like this would be a joy.* She shivered and checked her watch. It was almost 9:00— Nora walked back to the relative warmth of her car to wait for Sally.

Nora watched as Sally slowed her SUV in front of the Lucky Dragon. Sally turned the Sportage into the parking lot and parked beside Nora's car. The two women climbed from their vehicles and hugged.

"Thanks for meeting me," Nora said as she stepped back from the embrace. "I came by a little early to take another look at the building—it's so pretty."

"I know," Sally said. "I was just thinking the same thing as I turned the corner. I remember how happy I was when I first noticed the brick being painted lavender. And, it's amazing that the Wisteria is still blooming! Those flowers are as gorgeous as they are impossible at this time of year."

With those words the two women turned toward the building.

"My God, what happened!" cried Nora. The Lucky Dragon building that had moments ago glowed white in Nora's eyes was now weathered-red brick. It looked just as it had when Nora had first seen it, albeit a bit more shopworn and missing its Lucky Dragon neon sign.

"Oh, it's gone. My lovely lavender building is gone," Sally said, speaking to no one in particular. She turned to Nora. "Let's see if we can get in."

The sign on the scuffed front door read CLOSED. Not deterred, Nora pulled on the handle. The door didn't budge. Nora, again, put her nose to the now dirty window—the room was empty except for a few overturned tables and some boards leaning against the far wall where the fireplace had once blazed. "It's empty. . . it's all gone," Nora said.

"Not that I don't believe you, but can I have a look?" Sally asked. Nora stepped aside to let Sally peer in the window. "You're right—I think we're back to seeing the same thing. I don't think we need to tell LD anything—he obviously already knows we've decided to forgo our next wishes."

"I suppose you're right. He always did know what we were going to do—sometimes before we did. . . I really wish I could've gone back inside to sit by the fire, read a book, and pet the kitty. It was such a perfect bookstore—I would absolutely love to run a place like that someday."

"Who knows, maybe you will," Sally said. "Stranger things have happened."

Nora smiled. "You don't say. . ." she said, shaking her head.

As the two women turned to leave, a warm breeze—unusual on such a cold day—engulfed them. It smelled faintly of LD's expensive cigars.

CHAPTER 21 ~ SALLY

"Sally, listen to me, you have it all wrong," Bruce said while standing in front of the open garage door, boxes of his tailored shirts, golf trophies, and collectable liquor decanters filling the stall where he normally parked his Escalade. He had just come back from another "business trip to Duluth," and the long hours alone had given Sally the opportunity to pack his things and stack them toward the front of the garage door, effectively blocking his vehicle from entering. Sally thought of it as a *moat of junk*—her first line of defense. Bruce's garage door opener still worked, but she'd had the door locks changed. He could get into the garage after he moved his belonging, but he could no longer get into the house.

"What is it that I have wrong, Bruce? —that you don't have a branch office in Duluth or that you don't have a mistress? I have proof of both those things."

"No, Sal. It's not like that."

"Oh, also, since you borrowed money for your company from me under false pretenses, my lawyer tells me that besides divorcing you, I can charge you with fraud and theft."

"But—"

"*But*, nothing, Bruce—get your *butt* out of here and take your stuff with you. Whatever you don't take tonight gets donated to thrift stores—I know you'll just love that." Sally paused and then said, "Just do me one favor—don't tell the girls about us. I don't want to completely ruin their first Christmases away from home." Sally slammed the door and walked back into the kitchen. It was only then that she began to cry.

Trudy and her family had left on the Sunday after Thanksgiving, and Tiffany had taken off for Spain on December second. Sally had waited until her daughter was safely in Barcelona to pack Bruce's things, but she'd started preparing for his departure in between getting the girls' off to their new locales. She wasn't sure that she'd made the right decision in not telling them that she and their father were splitting up, but she also didn't want to take the shine off of their impending adventures. She hoped that Bruce would see the sense in waiting until the new year to tell the girls about the divorce—she hoped that she could trust him to stay quiet. She knew that both girls would take the split hard, especially Tiffany, but Sally had been living with Bruce's betrayal for almost two months—it was time. It wasn't like she was rushing into things. The affair was hurtful, but, perhaps, forgivable. Sally had always told herself if Bruce fooled around—but their life together remained unchanged—well, then, what was the harm? That notion had ended when she'd discovered that the $150,000 of her inheritance that Bruce had borrowed to cover the startup cost of the Duluth branch, had actually been used to fund his expensive trysts with the redhead. For some reason, lying about the money was more hurtful to Sally than the affair itself. It was as though he'd been stealing from her parents—and from his daughters. Sally couldn't live with that.

Sally needed someone to talk to, but she was sorely lacking friends in whom she could confide. Most of her acquaintances, except for a few neighbors and those at the thrift stores, she'd met through Bruce. And, even if those friends didn't take his side, discussing her marital problems with them would be awkward. So, two weeks before Christmas, when Nora called to ask if Sally would join her on an afternoon jaunt to Casket Arts, she jumped at the invitation. While Sally realized that Nora wouldn't be the ideal person for such a discussion, she and Nora had a special, if somewhat strange, bond. The younger woman would have to do.

"Thanks for picking me up," said Nora as she climbed into Sally's Sportage.

"Not a problem. I had to come this direction to get to Casket Arts anyway. It's a win-win—we'll have more time to talk, and we'll pollute the air just a little less."

Nora buckled her seatbelt and said, "I'll have to admit, talking is what I'm most interested in today—not to say we shouldn't pay attention to climate change, but I'm kinda focused on my own issues these days."

"Aren't we all. . ." sighed Sally as she pulled away from the curb.

"You too? Oh, I'm sorry—I forgot about your daughters leaving. Your youngest just left on that exchange trip to Europe, right?"

"Yeah—Spain, but that's only part of what's going on."

"So what else is happening? You're still feeling good, aren't you?"

"I feel great—it's my marriage that's falling apart. I found out some things about my husband, and, well, I kicked him out of the house."

"Oh, Sally—I'm so sorry."

"Yeah, me too. But you know, now that I've said it aloud to you, it doesn't strike me as such an awful thing. I'd been feeling alone for years—even when Bruce was in the house. Maybe it's going to be okay."

"Do your daughters know?" Nora asked as Sally made her way through the downtown Minneapolis traffic.

"No, not yet. I want to get through Christmas. I'm hoping Bruce won't spill the beans—he's not exactly trustworthy. I'd like it if the girls could enjoy the holiday without having to worry about us or feel as though they need to take sides."

"Yeah, that's tough. Unfortunately, I know way too much about what it's like to have friends taking sides in break-ups. I can't imagine how hard it would be for families."

"I hope we get through it. . . but enough about me, what's going on with you?"

Nora sighed heavily. "I'm just feeling so adrift right now. My jobs are dead ends, and without the wedding or any future plans, I don't really know what to do with myself. I'm starting to wonder if it was a good idea to give up my last two wishes."

"Well, what do you want to do? What was your dream when you were younger?" Sally asked.

"Other than getting married and having children, like most little girls who play with dolls?" Nora said, looking at Sally with a sideways glance.

"Other than that," Sally said nodding.

"I've always wanted to do something with books. That's why I was getting my master's in library science."

"Well, do you want to go back and finish your degree? You could do that, you know."

"I've thought about it, but I'm not sure I want to go into more debt. Plus, being a librarian turned out to be about a lot more than books. I'm embarrassed to admit that I didn't know that going in."

"So, what else could you do with books? Do you want to be an author?"

"Oh, goodness, no. I much prefer reading to writing. I like analyzing the worlds other people build rather than attempting to build my own." Nora reached over to the air vent and directed the warm blast away from her face.

"Okay, no writing, then." Sally said.

"To be honest, I can't get the cozy bookstore that Lucky D showed me out of my mind. I don't know the first thing about running a business, but I can't imagine ever having a bad workday if I were surrounded by books and fellow readers."

"Well, let's think on that one—" Sally said as she slammed on the brakes. "Did you see that? He blew right through that red light." Changing the subject, she continued, "How are things with your family? Have your mom's spirits improved now that you've paid them back for the wedding?"

"I *think* so. . ." Nora shrugged. "You may have figured out that my mom and I aren't all that good at talking to one another—not that I'm saying that you're old enough to be my mother, but maybe you could give me some motherly advice?"

"I'm not sure about me not being old enough to be your mom—how old are you, if you don't mind me asking?"

"No, it's okay—I'll be thirty-six in a month."

"You're the same age as my Trudy—so you're right, I'm not old enough to be your mom." Sally said as she turned from University onto 17th Avenue.

Nora cocked her head and squinted at Sally. "What's that supposed to mean?"

"I had Trudy when I was seventeen—not an ideal age for motherhood," Sally said. She continued, explaining about the car accident and her long recovery. ". . . So, Bruce took over as Trudy's father. He never formally adopted her, but he's been the only dad she's ever known."

"That makes me think of that wish-payment dream— the part about me being adopted," Nora said. "I'm dealing with the cancer part—I don't want to believe it, but I can. But how can it be that I'm nearly thirty-six-years-old and not know whether I'm adopted? That's completely nuts."

"Parents can do strange things in the name of protecting their children," said Sally, flipping on the signal before turning onto the street leading to D'Wight's studio.

"Yeah, I can see my mom keeping something like that from me. . . but my dad? I thought we were closer than that."

"Maybe you should ask him about it. I'm sure he wants to tell you. If that payment dream is what really happens on his deathbed, it must be weighing on him. If he says you weren't adopted, you can chalk his confession up to morphine. Anyway, I think you deserve to know. Especially if it will help you feel better," Sally said as she pulled into a parking spot on a residential street lined with mature trees near D'Wight's studio.

"Thanks, I think I do, too. Now, let's go see some art."

"Sally! Nora! Fantastic to see you!" D'Wight said as the two women entered the studio.

"Hi, D'Wight," Nora said, looking around. "Wow, there's so much more art in here than last time we visited. Do you ever sleep?"

"Sometimes, but I've been super inspired lately with this new space. I'm embarrassed to say that I've been sleeping on that couch more nights than in my bed," he flushed as he gestured to the worn plaid couch in the center of the room.

Nora smiled, "I don't think it's embarrassing. It's got to feel amazing, being so passionate about something."

"I guess I'm passionate about a lot of things—," D'Wight stopped talking. He raked his fingers through his hair and appeared to grasp for another topic. "—anyway, I think my cat might miss me. Although, I haven't actually seen her much lately. I never know where she goes."

"You have a cat? What does she look like?" Nora asked.

"Yeah, she was my parent's cat. She's been around forever," D'Wight pulled out his phone and scrolled. "Here she is. Her name is Eggroll," he said, holding up a photo of a calico cat identical to the cat Nora had met in the Lucky Dragon's bookstore.

"Well, I think she might start hanging around at your place again soon," Nora said.

Sally, who had walked away to look at D'Wight's art and give the two young people some space, gasped with pleasure as she rounded the corner of a room divider.

"Come, look at this piece, Nora!" Sally pointed toward a large ornate dragon made from hundreds of pieces of folded paper.

"That's my newest—my homage to the Lucky Dragon," D'Wight said.

"Ahh, yes, the Lucky Dragon. What's going on with the building these days? When I drove past it last week it was looking sort of rough," Sally said.

"Yeah, I don't know what's happening. I'm starting to think that the folks who bought it have changed their minds. Who knows, I might end up owning it again."

"Would that be so bad?" asked Nora, "You could move your studio into the space."

"No, not a chance—I like it here with the other artists. Besides, there aren't my kind of customers in that neighborhood. In this building, people are walking around expressly to look at and buy art. It makes a huge difference—more walk-in sales and fewer advertising expenses."

"What do you think you'll do with the Lucky Dragon if it comes back to you?" Sally asked, still examining the large origami assemblage.

"Rent it out, I guess," D'Wight said.

"Would you let me know if you get it back?—I might have some ideas for the space," Sally ventured.

"Sure, I want to keep living upstairs, but, yeah, the main floor has potential as a restaurant or a store—it could even be an office after some remodeling. But let's change the subject, okay? As far as I'm concerned, the Lucky Dragon is a next year problem. Or maybe it won't be a problem at all—I could be worrying for nothing."

"A next year problem—I like the way you think, D'Wight," Sally said. "I'm going to adopt your philosophy to use with the stuff that's been bothering me. No more worrying about it until next year. I'm going to enjoy this Christmas. How about you, Nora?"

"Me, what?" replied Nora, apparently distracted by her own concerns.

"No worrying until 2019—make everything that's bothering you right now a next year problem. Enjoy

Christmas—celebrate New Year's Eve like it's 1999!" D'Wight said.

Sally looked at D'Wight and laughed, "I would've never taken you for a Prince fan—aren't you a little young?"

"I'm a life-long Minnesotan—of course I'm a Prince fan. Do you think we listened to that piped-in Chinese Muzak shit when we cleaned the restaurant and prepped dumplings? No way—we had the *1999* and *Purple Rain* albums blasting."

"Party like it's 1999? Okay, you two—I'm in. I'm just going to enjoy life for a while—no worries until next year," Nora said.

"I'd say let's toast to it, but I don't have anything to drink in the studio."

"Sally and I are heading over to Northeast Social—you could join us there for a toast when you close up."

"Wish I could, but I keep late hours this time of year. Rain check?"

"You betcha," Nora replied, feigning a thick northern Minnesota accent.

The Christmas decorations that had been piled in the corner during Sally and Nora's last visit to Northeast Social now festooned the restaurant's mirror-backed bar and all of the deep windowsills above the banquette. The overly large hexagon-shaped light fixtures that already looked like they belonged in the Hogwarts's dining hall were now surrounded by floating candles suspended from the ceiling, lending the dimly lit room a festive Potterish charm. Sally watched as Nora beamed at the transformation.

"I just love Christmas decorations. They make everything so magical." Nora gushed.

"You haven't had enough magic for one year?" Sally asked.

"Not this kind—it's beautiful. You can't tell me that you don't like it."

"No, you're right. I like it, although I think the decorations look a bit odd on top of the normal Halloweeny vibe of this place." Sally saw the immediate disappointment in Nora's face so added, "But it's very well done—very. . . eerie-cheery."

Sally and Nora ordered hot spiced wine and toasted to not worrying about next year's problems. Following that, they toasted to D'Wight and his continued success in his new studio space.

"I wonder if he'll be getting the building back," Nora said.

"About that—I have an idea. Now, this is purely hypothetical, but I started thinking when D'Wight was talking about finding a tenant. What if we rent the space if he gets it back?"

"We? You and me?" Nora said, swirling the aromatic wine in her mug.

"Well, yes—but don't worry. Remember, no worrying—I'd foot the bill. What I'm thinking is, you should have your bookstore. I'd like a little space for a teashop toward the back, but the rest of the space would be for books, and you would run it."

"But, I've never—"

"But you could. I know you could. Think about it—the space is ideal. The foot traffic wouldn't be as good as some places in the city, but it's not bad. There are other shops in the area, and the building has a parking lot, which is a huge plus, and it's on the bus line—another plus."

"I know you never saw it like I did, but it was a great little bookstore," said Nora in a wistful tone.

"It was a perfect tea shop, too. So, what do you say— should we do some planning and talk to D'Wight?"

"I'm in if you think you can swing it—I can't—"

"Eh, eh, eh—no worrying, remember? I've got money and business experience—we just need your vision and book expertise. And, well, we need the space—but I have a hunch that Lucky D is done with it. I just hope that he's not done with us—the luck part, that is."

CHAPTER 22 ~ NORA

"One order of spaghetti and meatballs with extra sauce and a chicken parmesan. Is there anything else I can get you two?" Nora smiled at Dorothy and John as she set down their usual dinners.

"This is perfect, dear," said Dorothy. Nora began to walk away, but the regular put a hand on her arm. "Are you sure you're doing okay?" The couple, having missed their Saturday Gina's dates for a few weeks, had asked Nora about the wedding when they'd sat down. She told them briefly about the split with Brad. She'd gotten her elevator speech about being jilted down to a concise thirty seconds. It appeased most of her acquaintances, but Dorothy was a special case.

"Yes, I'm fine," Nora said, putting on her brightest fake smile.

"You may not believe it, but John and I both know about heartbreak," Dorothy said.

"Really? I thought you two were high school sweethearts," said Nora, confused about how this long-married couple could have a history of heartbreak.

"We were, but we didn't stay together after high school graduation," John said, cutting into his giant meatball.

"John went to the University of Minnesota here in the Twin Cities, while I went to St. Olaf College in Northfield. Distance wasn't the same back in those days. Neither of us had cars, and long-distance phone calls, even in the same state, cost a lot of money," Dorothy said.

"So, Dorothy and I both dated other people in college," John said after swallowing his bite.

"I was even briefly engaged to someone else. We didn't get as far as you and Brad, but it almost happened. I'm so glad I experienced that heartache, because it meant I was able to reconnect with John after college graduation and have the wonderful life we've built for the last 46 years." Dorothy reached out to clasp John's hand across the table.

"Wow, that's quite a story," Nora said.

"I have a feeling you've got a future waiting for you that's better than you could ever imagine," said John. "This is a beginning, not an ending."

"You know, I think you might be right," Nora said, with a real smile this time.

~

On Sunday morning, Nora walked into Melanie's foyer laden with Christmas gifts for Melanie and Juliet, plus the customary bottle of Maker's Mark that she gave to Melanie's husband every year.

"Merry Christmas, Bunny," Melanie said, taking half of the gifts from Nora's arms and leading her to the Christmas tree.

"Merry Christmas, Kitty." Nora placed the gifts under the tree in the living room and the old college roommates embraced. "Where's Juliet?"

"She's spending some quality time with her daddy. Crazy man—I think he took her Christmas shopping, or maybe they went to the conservatory at Como Park. It's so nice there in the winter." At that, Melanie took hold of Nora's upper arms and looked her in the face. "Now, how are you? And don't you dare say 'fine' again. I want to know how you're really doing."

"I'm… at peace, I think. At least with the breakup. The more I think about it, the more I think Brad really wasn't the right person for me," Nora said.

"Oh, thank goodness. I'm so glad to hear that." Melanie let go of Nora's arms. "I never want to be the kind of person who says, 'I told you so,' but I do think this is for the best. Now, can I get you something to drink?"

"Do you really have to ask?" Nora said with a smile.

"Good point—one coffee with cream, coming right up," Melanie said as she ducked into the kitchen.

Nora wandered around the living room looking at books and artwork. A photo of Nora and Melanie taken at their college graduation sat on a bookcase shelf alongside some of their favorite books. Nora picked up the framed picture—the girls in the photo looked so young, so totally unaware of what life had in store for them, yet excited to experience whatever it was going to be. It made Nora feel nostalgic for that time and that friendship.

Melanie came back into the room holding two mugs. "Oh, I love that photo of us. It always makes me think of sunny days hanging out on the quad with you," Melanie said while setting the mugs on the coffee table.

Nora put down the photo and went to sit on the couch. "Hey, can we talk about something before we open presents?" she asked.

"Of course. What's up? If it's about me saying that the breakup was for the best. . . " Melanie grimaced.

"No, no, I think you're right about that. It's just that after spending the afternoon together on my not wedding day, it made me realize how much I miss you. I miss all the fun we used to have. Can we spend more time together? Obviously, I know Juliet will likely need to be with us, but

I'd be happy to get coffee and bring it over. Or we can go walk around Lake of the Isles with her stroller when it gets nice again. I just miss you Kitty. . . I miss my best friend."

"Yes, absolutely! I've missed you so much. Being a mom is so much more isolating than I thought it would be."

"Even with your mom friend, Darcy?" Nora said, thinking of the flawless blonde at Juliet's birthday party.

"Honestly? She kind of drives me crazy sometimes. Don't get me wrong, it's nice having another mom to talk to but she's just. . . too perfect, you know? It's a lot to measure up to."

"Oh, I totally understand—I can promise you I won't be perfect. And, while I'm glad you have someone to talk with about being a mom, you'll always have me for everything else, okay?"

"Thank you," Melanie said. She smiled and hugged Nora once more. "Can we open presents now?"

"Absolutely!"

~

Nora sat in the breakroom at Mill City Physical Therapy, scraping the bottom of her yogurt container. Her lunch break was almost over when her phone screen lit up and read MESSAGE FROM D'WIGHT WONG. Nora felt her pulse spike as she unlocked her phone to read the text.

D'WIGHT WONG: Hey Nora! I hope it's okay that I'm texting. I was wondering if you and Sally wanted to come over to my place for dinner tomorrow night? I'm going to make Sally's favorite pork cutlets and gravy… if you like pork, that is. If you don't like pork, I can make something else. Anyway, let me know. ☺

Well, it wasn't a date, but it was another chance to see D'Wight. Plus, she and Sally could scout out the Lucky Dragon space. If it wasn't being worked on, maybe it would be coming back into D'Wight's possession soon. Nora still couldn't believe that Sally would be willing to foot the bill for a bookstore if they could lease the building.

NORA WANAMAKER: I'd love to! And, yes, I like pork. ☺ Let me know what time. I can bring a bottle of wine.

~

"Let me take your coats while you catch your breath. I know most people aren't used to hiking up twenty-two steps to enter an apartment. I've done it all my life, so I don't think about it. Sorry," D'Wight said as he took Sally and Nora's coats and hung them on a hall tree just off the landing.

D'Wight's apartment above the Lucky Dragon was both charming and cluttered. *This apartment is a dream*, Nora thought. She loved the old, polished wood floors, big windows, and exposed brick. A fire blazed in the fireplace on the wall across from the staircase, making the room flicker golden.

"Your place is fantastic," Nora said.

"Agreed!" Sally added.

"Thanks, I like it. It's home. Like I said, I've lived here all my life. My sisters couldn't wait to leave—both our home and the restaurant—but I've always had a hard time imagining my days anywhere else. At least the home part."

"Could you show us around?" asked Sally. "If you wouldn't mind."

"No, not at all. I even cleaned, thinking you might ask."

D'Wight showed Sally and Nora around the three-bedroom apartment that he had decorated with his artist's eye and craftsman's touch.

"So, here's where you put the Lucky Dragon sign," Sally said, examining the neon sign up close for the first time. The sign dominated the wall beside the fireplace with its depiction of a mirth-filled dragon smoking a cigar and rolling dice.

"Yes, well, it was my first foray into commercial art—my parents let me design their new logo when I was fifteen. It was such a rush to see it mounted on the outside of the restaurant. It was like they were saying that they believed in me—my art was good enough to be taken seriously. . . I miss them. . ."

"They sound like special people—good parents," Nora said.

"They were. Not perfect—but good."

Sally responded, "That's all a parent can hope to be. I just hope my daughters feel the same way about me."

"How could they not?" D'Wight said.

"You're sweet, and now, before I blush, I'm going to change the subject—where does that door go? Is it another bathroom?" Sally asked.

"Nope, only one bathroom. It's the door to the back stairs—they go to the hallway beside the restaurant kitchen. They're kinda narrow and winding, but those are the steps we always used before I sold the building. At first it felt really strange to use the front stairs."

"Oh, I get it—who comes in the front door of their own house?" Nora said.

"Queqie de," D'Wight replied.

"Pardon?" Nora said.

"Oh, it's just something my parents said—it means "exactly," or at least that's what I think it means. My Mandarin's a bit iffy."

"Could we open the door—sneak a peek?" asked Sally who appeared to have been lost in her own thoughts.

"At the stairs? Sure, but they're gonna be dusty—I don't clean what I don't see."

"That's not a problem. Do you think we could take a look at the main floor, too—if you don't think we'd be trespassing. . ."

"We'd be trespassing, but I haven't heard any noise from down there for weeks, so I doubt we'll get caught. We can take a quick look—just promise you won't tell anyone."

"You got it," Sally said and pantomimed zipping her mouth closed.

"The way things look, it might be mine again after January first, anyway," D'Wight said.

Sally looked at Nora standing behind D'Wight. Nora held up her hand and crossed her fingers in a hopeful gesture.

"What a dusty mess," said D'Wight as they stood in what used to be the main dining room of the Lucky Dragon. "I'm glad my parents can't see it like this. It would break their hearts."

"What? It not being a restaurant?" Nora asked.

"No, not that so much. Just being a mess and sorta being in limbo—my parents hated waste. They woulda just hated seeing the building not making money."

Sally had been walking around the gutted space, paying little attention to D'Wight and Nora's conversation. She cleared her throat and motioned toward a wall of scuffed Sheetrock. "Is it possible that there's a fireplace behind here?"

"I don't ever remember seeing one, but maybe." D'White walked over and knocked on the wall in several places. "Hear that? Sounds like a drum—it's right below the fireplace in my living room, so, it makes sense. If I get the property back, I'll take a sledgehammer to the drywall and we'll know for sure."

"About getting the building back—" said Sally before being cut-off by D'Wight.

"I promise, you'll be the first to know, and I also promise to give you a sweet deal if you want to rent it."

With that remark, Nora finally uncrossed the fingers on her left hand that she'd been hiding in her jeans pocket the whole time the trio had been inspecting the main floor.

~

"Dinner was delicious, D'Wight. I'd love to repay your kindness. . . Are you doing anything on Christmas Day?" Sally asked.

"Just early—I go over to watch my nephews tear into their gifts from Santa, but then they go to their dad's family's Christmas. So, yeah, I'm free all afternoon."

"Would you like to join me for Christmas dinner? I'm a little short on family this year," Sally said. "Would you like to come, too?" Sally asked Nora.

"That's sweet of you, Sally, but I've been planning on spending the day with my parents."

"Do you think that they'd consider coming to my place for dinner? All three of you?" Sally asked in a hopeful tone.

"I know that my mom would absolutely love an invitation, and Dad, well, he'll do whatever mom tells him to. So, while I can't say for certain, it's likely. But you'll have to call them—Mom will need to hear the invitation from you."

"I'd love to include your parents. I'll call this evening. After so many years of cooking holiday meals for a crowd, it's easier for me to cook a big meal than a small one." Looking at both Nora and D'Wight, Sally continued, "Any food allergies I should know about—likes or dislikes?"

"None for me! I eat everything," D'Wight said and patted his non-existent belly.

Their meal over, D'Wight helped Sally with her coat and handed her a bag of crab rangoon to-go.

"Nora, come down in about five or ten minutes—it'll take at least that long for me to get the car cleaned off and the engine warmed," Sally said with a surreptitious wink, before turning to walk down the stairs from D'Wight's apartment.

"Sally's so nice. She makes me feel a little guilty. I'm probably the one who should be clearing snow off the car," Nora said.

"No—she's just been a mom too long. Always wanting to help people younger than herself—my mom was the same way. She bought my underwear until I was, well, far too old to be having my mom buy my underwear," D'Wight said and immediately turned red, perhaps realizing the awkwardness of discussing his underwear with Nora.

"Right—" Nora replied, slightly jarred by the thought of a grown-up D'Wight in Underoos.

D'Wight lifted Nora's heavy jacket from the hall tree and held it while she put her arms through the sleeves. He stood quietly watching as Nora buttoned her coat, wrapped her scarf around her neck and slipped on her mittens. Once she'd finished, he spoke. "This might sound crazy, but would you want to go out sometime after Christmas? I know you just broke up with your fiancé, and it's probably way too soon, and I don't even know if you like me like that, but I just had to ask."

Nora's first reaction, after suppressed excitement, was remembering seeing D'Wight's partially clad hug in the parking lot on the day she'd attempted to return her wedding dress to the bridal store. "I'd like to go out with you, but I got the impression that you have a girlfriend. I don't want to get into the middle of anything—"

"No—what would give you that idea?" D'Wight interrupted.

"Just something I saw," said Nora, attempting to sound dispassionate.

"Come on, Nora, be more specific. I'd know if I had a girlfriend."

"Okay—I saw you hugging a woman in your parking lot—and it kinda looked like you had just rolled out of bed," Nora said rather sheepishly.

"So, what did this woman look like? I've gotta figure this out."

"She was petite with really long black hair—I couldn't really see her face, but I remember you weren't wearing much—not even shoes."

"Nora, that was my big sister. Her name's Iris—she dropped by that morning with some brownies she'd just baked. I remember because she gave me hell for following her outside without shoes."

"Oh," Nora responded, sounding even more sheepish.

"So, now that we've got my relationship status straightened out, would you consider going out with me, Nora Wanamaker?"

"Yes, I would, D'Wight Wong." Nora said, all her sheepishness gone.

"Okay! Great!" D'Wight shoved a bag of egg rolls into Nora's bemittened hands. As she descended the stairs, Nora glanced backward to see D'Wight still holding the

door open and grinning from his chin to his shaggy black
bangs.

CHAPTER 23 ~ SALLY

"Merry Christmas, James," Sally said as she walked up to the checkout counter at Second Chances Thrift Store. In one hand, she carried a wide, hard-bottomed bag, keeping it as parallel to the store's floor as two lines on staff paper.

"What can I do ya for today, Sally? Buying, donating, or both, like usual?" James replied.

"Would you believe none of the above? Today I'm handing out checks. Will you please see that the hospice office gets this?" Sally reached into her tote and handed James a check for $1,000 and a plate of homemade cookies. "The check, that is; the cookies are for you and Tom if he's working today."

"Wow—thank you!" James said, looking at the check. "Tom's here—out back if ya wanna say hi."

"I don't have anything to donate today, but I'd like to wish him Merry Christmas."

"Sure thing, Sally—and thanks for the cookies. I'll make sure that the money gets to where it needs to go."

Sally walked to the back of the store and knocked on the door labeled "Employees Only."

When Tom answered, Sally wished him a happy holiday and told him about the cookies she'd left with James. "The other thing that I wanted to tell you is that I won't be coming by as often as I have in the past—I've decided to give up the color distribution system and just give money to the charities I support."

"We'll miss you Sally—James and I agree, you're one of the *strangest*, err, I mean *nicest*, people we know. But I thought you liked all that color sorting. Why're you quitting?"

"I have enjoyed it, but I've been learning that there's a season for everything—I'm ready for a change. I've started focusing on the piano again, and I might have a whole new project this coming year. If that happens, I'm going to be very busy."

"Well, best of luck to you, and Merry Christmas," Tom said as Sally walked out the door.

After dropping off a check and cookies at Treasure Trove and letting the staff know that she would no longer be seeing them weekly, Sally drove to the Lucky Dragon. Slowing her Sportage to a crawl, she noted that winter winds had blown leaves and fast-food wrappers into the entry area by the front door. The forlorn brick building appeared to be suffering from owner neglect. *Oh, I hope D'Wight gets the building back*, thought Sally. She missed the lavender exterior and the blooming window boxes. Not that it would look that way if she and Nora leased the building, but she knew that they could definitely make it an inviting space. With even a modicum of care, it couldn't help but look a lot better than it did right now.

Sally shook her head, stepped on the gas, and hurried toward St. Paul. She had a delivery to make to Twice Nice before going to the store to buy the things she'd need for a holiday dinner for five. The sooner she got to Kowalski's, the better—this close to Christmas, the grocery store was sure to be crowded.

~

As the clock in the front hall chimed twelve times, Sally finished wrapping the banister with a heavy evergreen garland. *It's Christmas Eve Day*, she thought. After putting away her groceries, she had spent all afternoon and evening festooning the house. She hadn't planned on going to all the fuss of decorating this year, assuming she'd be the only person around to appreciate it, but, once she'd invited company for Christmas dinner, she felt she owed it to her guests. Besides, she had never met an adult who seemed to like holiday decorations more than Nora. *After everything she's been through lately, Nora deserves some joy.* Sally hoped that Nora was keeping her promise to stay worry free until the new year—*I wish the poor girl could just enjoy life for a little while. . .*

Sally turned off the living room lights and flopped on the couch. The colored lights on the tree in the corner and the clear bulbs buried within the stairway garland brightened the winter night. She should have been exhausted after her long day, but instead, she felt an energized contentment. Having been granted good health and her ability at the piano—well, it was as if she'd been given a new lease on life at the age of fifty-two. And, though she missed her family, she'd learned that she didn't miss the day-to-day responsibility of caring for them. She thought of the loads of laundry that she didn't have to wash, dry, and fold and the meals she no longer needed to prepare, serve, and clear. And, yes, she missed her grandsons, but she didn't miss wrangling their twisting torsos into snowsuits or the challenge of having to corral and wrestle two kicking toddlers into car seats. A new equation had taken over her life:

Health + artistic purpose + freedom = JOY!

She stretched her body until her toes touched the end of the couch and then pulled the fuzzy wool afghan to her chin. Sally fell asleep under the glow of the Christmas lights while thinking of possibilities for the future.

~

"Merry Christmas, D'Wight! Let me take your coat," said Sally. "Nora and her folks aren't here yet, but I expect them shortly. Did you have any problems finding the place?"

"Nope, just plugged your address into GPS—it directed me right to your driveway."

"Yeah, guess that's a stupid question anymore. My age is showing."

"Anything but—I don't know if it's my place to say this, but you seem to be growing younger every time I see you. I hate to think that it's because you gave up eating food from the Lucky Dragon."

"Aww, thanks, D'Wight—I'll take that as a compliment, and, no, I don't think it's from a change in diet. I miss your food. It could be from some other life changes, though."

"Well, you should bottle whatever it is— hey, I think I just heard a car pull in."

Sally opened the front door expecting to see Nora and her parents, instead she saw Bruce walking up the incline of the driveway. Neither Bruce nor Sally said a word until Bruce reached the front door.

"I see you have a *friend* visiting—" Bruce blurted while looking past Sally at D'Wight standing in the foyer. "Suppose you two'd like to be left *alone*."

"Well, Merry Christmas to you, too. . ." Sally said, pausing and refraining from calling Bruce the descriptor that had crossed her mind. "D'Wight's a friend. Unlike you, I don't fu— I don't *date* friends who are decades younger than me. What do you want Bruce—why are you here?"

"Damned if I know, Sally—I thought you might want company on Christmas."

"I have company, Bruce. And you should move your car because the other people I've invited for dinner will want that spot—I told them to park in *my* driveway."

Bruce turned and walked toward the Escalade, climbed in, and backed out so quickly he nearly hit the Wanamaker's car as it inched down the street, its three occupants attempting to read house numbers obscured by Christmas decorations.

Sally turned toward D'Wight, "Sorry—he's probably just upset that he wasn't able to swoop in and save me to score some points in his favor. It's kind of a long-established pattern between us—maybe as much my doing as his. I'm sorry you got in the middle," Sally said.

"No, Sally, I'm sorry you had to go through it," replied D'Wight.

"It's okay—I found it strangely cathartic—especially the part where Bruce seemed to assume you were my boyfriend."

"That was kinda funny—no offense, but Nora's more my type."

"None taken, and you have good taste. I've got my fingers crossed for you two—" Sally said as Nora stepped from the back door of her parent's car, revealing a fitted red sweater and a vintage A-line green, red, and gold plaid skirt beneath her open dress coat, "—You might want to close your mouth before they come in, though."

D'Wight quickly closed his gaping mouth and smiled at Sally before he turned his gaze to Nora as she led her family up the brick walkway toward Sally's front door.

"Nora, you look like Christmas personified!" Sally said, welcoming Deb, Jim, and Nora into the house and hanging their coats in the entryway closet. Deb checked her hair in the mirror by the door and exclaimed, "This *is* a Home Interior's mirror—I recognize it! I always wanted one like this but settled for a smaller version."

Nora was the next Wanamaker to speak, "Your home is gorgeous, Sally. And the way you've decorated it—I feel like we've just stepped into the December issue of *Better*

Homes and Gardens magazine. You have such a fantastic staircase, and that garland—it's beautiful! It would be so much fun to live in a house like this."

"I was really happy when we found this place. I fell for it on first sight—thankfully, we had what we needed to purchase it. I often think about how this house was a good thing that came from a bad thing," Sally said.

"Don't tell me you're a bank robber," Jim quipped.

"No, nothing like that. It's just that Bruce and I had never owned a home until this one; we'd always rented. Nearly every extra dime went into growing Bruce's first liquor business. But my mother passed away shortly before we moved to Minnesota, so I inherited the family home— I am, or I was, an only child. Anyway, long story short, all of a sudden we had enough in the bank to buy a house in Edina."

"You chose well, Sally. It's a lovely home," Deb said.

"Would you like to see the rest of it? I only offer because I enjoy looking at houses when I visit people." Sally smiled at D'Wight, recalling Nora's and her visit to his apartment.

The three Wanamakers and D'Wight followed Sally through the first and second floors of the substantial Tudor-style home. Deb and Nora oohed and aahed over the woodwork, coffered ceilings, and custom drapes. Jim didn't say much until the group stepped into the upstairs hallway and he spotted Trudy's graduation picture hanging with several other Munson family portraits. "Why do you have a picture of Nora on your wall?"

"What?" replied Sally.

"That picture—I know it's not her, but it looks so much like Nora when she was a teenager," Jim said.

"Oh, that's my oldest daughter's graduation picture. Her name's Trudy, and it's funny you should mention the likeness. I don't know what she looked like as a teen, but the very first time I saw Nora—I honked at her—I thought she was Trudy."

"It's uncanny how much they look alike. They could be sisters. . ." Jim muttered, shaking his head.

"Maybe they're long-lost cousins—we'll have to compare our family histories," Sally said.

Before Jim could respond, Deb spoke up, "Oh, I very much doubt it—that won't be necessary. Let's go have a look at your Christmas tree. Do you do a theme tree? I love theme trees."

D'Wight pushed his chair from the table. "This was a great meal, Sally. Thank you so much for inviting me. To show you my thanks, let me clean up."

"No D'Wight, the kitchen's a mess—"

"More reason to let me do it. I've known my way around a messy kitchen since I learned to walk."

"I can help him," volunteered Nora, tilting her head and giving Sally a look that said—*If you're really my friend, you'll get out of the way and take my parents with you.*

"Jim, Deb—would you like to go to the living room and wait while I introduce these two to my kitchen? I'll put on a pot of decaf and join you shortly." As she said "shortly," Sally gave Nora a knowing glance.

Nora and D'Wight followed Sally, all three laden with dirty dishes, into the kitchen. Once they'd unburdened themselves, D'Wight turned to the women and said, "I think I have some news that you two will want to hear, but I wasn't sure if I should share it in front of your parents, Nora. But, anyway, it looks like I'm getting my building back. The investment group wants out of our contract for deed, so if you still want the building—"

"YES!" Sally and Nora said in unison.

"Okay, message received—the building is mine again as of January first. Sally, maybe we can get together and hash things out sometime this coming week if you're ready."

"You bet," replied Sally while Nora looked on, a huge grin filling her face.

Sally showed D'Wight and Nora the features of the dishwasher and told them to load it any way they saw fit. She asked them to hand-wash the cut-glass goblets and motioned to the cupboard where she kept the pots and pans. Sally started the Mr. Coffee, then headed to the living room. She entered just in time to hear Deb scolding Jim:

"Boy, I understand why you're such a lousy poker player—your face doesn't hide anything—when you saw that picture in the hallway you might as well have just shouted to everyone that Nora was adopted."

"I didn— Oh, hi Sally. Did you get the KP squad going?" Jim said in a clumsy attempt to change the subject.

"They're working away." Sally paused, but then spoke before she chickened out, "Deb, did I hear you say that Nora's adopted?"

"No, no—you, you must have misunderstood—" stammered Deb.

Jim hissed at his wife, "Stop it, Deb—it's time to admit it. There's no shame. It's time we tell people." He turned to Sally, "We adopted Nora when she was a week old. We always assumed that we would tell her when she was old enough to understand, but we just never did." Jim shook his head. "Now it seems too late."

Deb stood glaring at Sally and her husband, her lips pressed in an unforgiving line. When she finally broke her silence, she said, "Sally, don't tell anyone. Especially Nora."

"I wouldn't dream of telling Nora, it's not my information to share. But I do think you should tell her. She's certainly old enough to know, and from the little I've seen of your relationship, I doubt that it will make any difference in the way she feels about the two of you. You are her parents—she loves you."

"What do you know about how an adoptee would feel?" Deb shot back.

"Maybe more than you think. My oldest daughter isn't my soon-to-be ex-husband's biological child. Trudy was in kindergarten when Bruce and I married. He didn't formally adopt her, but she took his name and has been his daughter since the day we married. Bruce's and my marriage may be broken, but I don't think his bond with his daughters—both his daughters—will ever change."

"I think you're right," said Jim. "I think we should tell Nora."

"We'll see," said Deb with a tone that said *just as soon as the Vikings win the Super Bowl.*

CHAPTER 24 ~ NORA

The Monday after New Year's Day, Nora made the trek to her parents' suburban home to help her father take down the outdoor Christmas decorations. Deb always insisted that they be removed the day following Epiphany, the last of the twelve days of Christmas. Never mind that they lived in Minnesota, and January seventh was usually as cold as a snowman's nose. Nora was finishing her last task— removing the pinecones and bows from the shedding swags that had been hung beside the front door and shoving their dead boughs into the compost bag—when Jim solemnly asked her to follow him to the kitchen. She stood on the back door rug, her coat and mittens smelling of the damp cold, and knocked her boots together to clear the clinging snow. "Why so serious, Dad?" Nora asked.

"I've got to tell you something and I'd like to do it before your mom gets home. It's long overdue," Jim said. Nora's heart squeezed, thinking of his deathbed confession she'd seen in her payment to the Lucky Dragon. *So, was it real?*

"Well, say it quickly then—make it like pulling off a Band-Aid. You know, speed makes everything easier." Nora tried not to play her hand. She was assuming her father was going to tell her about being adopted, but in truth, she had no idea why he had invited her to the kitchen.

"Okay, I hope speaking quickly makes it less painful, too—Nora, you're adopted. I've wanted to tell you for so long now. Your mother and I adopted you when you were only a week old. I'm so sorry we never told you, but—" Jim's voice cracked, and he covered his face with his hands.

"Oh, Daddy, please don't cry. . ." Nora said, taking her father's hands from his face and holding them in hers. "It's okay, I've suspected it for years," Nora lied. "So, maybe I'm complicit—I've never asked you or Mom about it either. Daddy, it doesn't change how I feel about you. You're my dad and mom's my mom—hearing that I'm adopted doesn't change that."

"But how could you have known? Did someone say something?" Jim asked, not letting go of Nora's hands. "Did Sally tell you?"

"Sally? Sally Munson?—No, it was cousin Greg," Nora said, launching into the story she had concocted in hopes that this day would come. "When we were kids, he used to tease me all the time about not being a real Wanamaker. I thought he was just jealous because Grandma and Grandpa used to let me stay overnight at their house, but they'd never invite the boy cousins to stay. One day, when we were all together, I heard Grandma get really mad at Greg for his taunting—I don't think she knew that I heard her, but something about the way she said what she said made me think there was truth to the teasing."

"But you never said anything to us. Why, honey?"

"Maybe for the same reason you and Mom didn't tell me—I didn't know how, and it really didn't matter to me." Nora said, now crying, too.

Deb walked into the kitchen bundled in her winter coat, carrying bags of groceries. Nora and Jim had been so lost in their conversation that they had failed to hear the garage door open and close. "Thanks for undecorating the house you two," Deb said as she set the bags on the counter. That must have been when she noticed the tears on Jim and Nora's faces. "Jim? What did you do? Jim?"

"He told me, Mom. It's okay," Nora said, wiping her still rosy nose with a sleeve.

Instead of responding to her daughter, Deb glared at Jim. "I thought we'd agreed—"

Jim interrupted, "I didn't agree to anything. It was time for Nora to know. Now she does. Truth is, she already did."

"Sally said she'd keep her mouth shut," Deb hissed.

"Mom, it wasn't Sally—why would you two even think that?"

"Who then? Who told you?"

"Well, no one told me directly. But, like I already told Dad, Cousin Greg used to tease me about not being a 'real' Wanamaker. He said it so often I started to think that there was something to it. Then one day I heard Grandma hushing him—from what she said to him, I figured it was true," Nora shrugged.

Deb looked at Jim, "Your mother—your mother let it slip?"

"Oh, don't blame Grandma—she didn't know that I heard her. She was scolding Greg—I wasn't meant to hear any of it."

"I never liked that kid," Deb said.

"Well, that makes two of us," Nora said, smiling through her tears.

Deb began taking groceries from the bag and putting them in the refrigerator, talking but not making eye contact with her husband or daughter. "I suppose you are going to try to find your birth family now."

"I don't know, Mom. I mean I just found out. . ." Nora said.

"Would that be so bad, Deb? We're getting older and we don't have much for extended family," Jim said. "If you don't count Greg, Nora only has two cousins."

"I don't know what I'll do—I need some time to think about it," Nora said.

"Well, just don't think you're going to find a bunch of brothers and sisters—from what I remember, your birth parents died in an accident right after you were born. I suppose they had parents and, maybe, brothers and sisters, but I would imagine they'll be pretty hard to find after all this time. They weren't even from Minnesota—"

"Why are you always so negative," Jim said.

"I'm not negative. I'm just being realistic. Dead couples don't have children, and it's been nearly thirty-six years. I don't want to give her hope." Deb slammed a can of tomato soup on the kitchen counter and began to cry.

Nora walked over, put her arms around Deb's thin shoulders, and gently hugged her. "Mom, you're the only mother I care about. If I decide to look for any other relatives, I'll let you know, I promise. Right now it's not important to me, but I am glad Daddy told me. It's something I should know about myself."

Deb put her head on Nora's shoulder and sighed. "I suppose you're right."

ACT III

The Happily Ever After

CHAPTER 25 ~ SALLY

Sally stood on the rolling ladder and stapled a temporary cardboard label reading *Magical Realism* above the top shelf in the stack. "No one but us is going to understand how appropriate this section is to our store," Sally said.

"You're right," said Nora, "and no one ever will." She pushed a wide construction broom down the aisle between the tall, free-standing bookcases. The bookstore was far from complete, but Sally and Nora had opted to keep construction costs down by being their own cleaning crew.

"I talked with the foreman—he said that by next week it'll be warm enough to start work on the exterior of the building," Sally said.

"Thanks for agreeing to paint the building white. I think you're going to like the finished look."

"I'm sure I will—I loved the computer rendering of your vision."

"Thank LD for that. I'm just having the painter recreate the building the way I saw it in November—down to the window boxes full of ferns. I was happy that D'Wight seemed to approve of the changes." Nora leaned the broom on an empty bookcase and retrieved a large dustpan. She held it to the floor next to the pile of construction debris so that Sally could easily sweep the mess over the pan's beveled edge.

"Nora, you've got to know by now that D'Wight's going to like anything you do—I don't know if I've ever met a man who wanted to please a woman more than D'Wight wants to please you."

"You think?" Nora replied glancing upward at Sally with a Mona Lisa smile on her face. Her eyes shined with delight at the thought of their new landlord.

The women continued to work in silence, clearing the dust, trash, and soda cans left by the construction crew, until Sally announced that she thought it was time for a break. She poured two mugs of coffee from a thermos sitting on the new stainless-steel counter in the back corner of the store. Nora joined her, pulling a couple of dingy folding chairs up to a table made from a sheet of plywood atop two sawhorses.

"This is going to be a nice little coffee space once we have some real tables and chairs," Nora said.

"Hey, it already is. I'm really glad you talked some sense into me and we scaled back my tea shop idea. I think the way things are working out, smaller is better. When I first thought about it, I hadn't counted on needing to—no, make that *wanting* to—practice so much. The piano is a demanding mistress to master."

"Clever, Sally, but I think the word 'master' is being cancelled? It has bad connotations historically."

"Thanks for the heads-up. It's funny you mention it—after I said it, I was questioning my use of the word 'mistress.' It has some recent bad connotations for me."

"No doubt," Nora responded looking up from scrolling on her phone. "Sorry to change the subject so abruptly, but I forgot to tell you, I've been trying to find some information about my birth parents."

"Really?" Sally replied. "I didn't think you were interested."

"Yeah, originally I hadn't planned on looking—it seemed pointless after my mom told me their lawyer had said both my parents died in a car accident right after I was born. But then I started thinking, maybe my mom had just wanted to put an end to the discussion. I figured that I could at least find out their names. . . I've requested copies of newspapers from around the day I was born."

"Were they local?" Sally asked while blowing on the steam still rising from her coffee.

"No. Mom and I finally talked a little more after she apologized for having kept things secret for so long—she told me she thought my birth parents were from western Iowa or eastern South Dakota. That's your part of the world, right? I'm having library searches done in the Sioux City Journal and the Sioux Falls Argus Leader. I figure one of those papers would've printed something about a fatal accident involving a young couple."

"You'd sure think so. . ." mused Sally. "Let me know what you learn—considering the area, we might actually be distantly related."

~

Sally paused mid-song and walked from the piano to her phone lying on the kitchen counter. *I really should start carrying this thing with me like everyone else does,* she thought as she picked up her ringing cell phone. "Hi Nora, what's up?"

"I just wanted to tell you what I found out from those newspaper searches I had done. It was kinda disappointing. Makes me wonder why I even bothered."

"They didn't find anything?" Sally asked.

"Not in the Sioux City paper, and only one story showed up in the Sioux Falls paper. It was about a bad crash involving two young people. They were around the right age, but neither of them died. Nothing was mentioned about a baby. I don't think it could be them."

"What were their names? If they were young in the early 80s, maybe I knew them—South Dakota isn't a very big state."

Sally listened to Nora flipping papers. "Here it is—the guy's name was Bentley Bradley and the girl was Sara Johnson. It says that they were both badly injured and in critical condition. Nothing was said about a baby being in the car or that this Sara person was pregnant, so I don't think it could be them."

"Your right about that," said a bewildered Sally. "That article's about me. My name is—was—Sara Johnson. My boyfriend was Ben Bradley. . . he died after the accident—in Rochester, I think. . . Trudy was delivered by emergency c-section right after. . ." Sally's voice trailed off as she thought about what Nora had said.

"God, this is weird. What's it all mean?" Nora asked.

"I don't know. . . but, maybe. . . maybe, the adoption agency lied? The baby—you—came from somewhere else, and Ben's and my car accident seemed like a good cover story. . . that's my guess, anyway."

"Are you saying something illegal happened?"

"No. . . not necessarily. . . just that the baby's mother—or, her family—wanted to keep the pregnancy and adoption private."

"Maybe I should just let them. I'm ready to quit looking—it's been thirty-six years now. I have parents I love, and I have a lot more important things to focus on in the next few months."

~

Sally couldn't get the phone conversation with Nora out of her head. There were too many pieces that seemed like they should lead to answers, but instead, led to more questions. It was like putting one of those new PuzzleTwist jigsaw puzzles together—the pieces fit, but the finished product didn't match the picture on the box lid.

Sally pondered, *who might be around to help answer my questions?* Her mother and father were both dead, and she hadn't seen or heard from Ben's mother since the accident. Her only hope was her Aunt Lois, her father's sister, whom everyone called Lodie. She had to be in her late eighties, but as far as Sally knew, still had most of her marbles. . . Perhaps it was time to take a break from sweeping sawdust and practicing the piano to make the four-and-a-half-hour drive to South Dakota.

~

"I'm sorry, Sally. I should have never waited this long to tell you, but your mother didn't want you to know—and well, I was sorta scared of her." Sally's Aunt Lodie squirmed in the plasticized nursing home chair. "She was a formidable woman, your mother."

"That she was," agreed Sally. "But thanks for telling me now."

Aunt Lodie had just told Sally that Trudy was not the only baby that Sally had given birth to after the accident. Trudy'd had a fraternal twin. Sally's parents, overwhelmed by the prospect of caring for two babies and, possibly, a brain-injured daughter, had arranged for one of the baby girls—the one that they'd named Nora—to be placed with an out-of-state family. It was to be a very private and very closed adoption. And, as far as Sally's mother was concerned, all who knew—and, she had made sure that there weren't many—were sworn to secrecy.

By the time she'd confronted her Aunt Lodie, Sally wasn't surprised by what her aunt had told her. Over the preceding days, when she'd thought about the resemblance between Nora and Trudy and the unexplainable things said by the ICU nurse and by her father on his deathbed, it all finally fell into place. She'd given birth to twins; Nora Wanamaker was her biological daughter.

How was she going to tell Nora and her other daughters? *It's all so strange. . . and, yet,* thought Sally—with a grin the size of Lake Superior on her face— *all so wonderful, too!*

CHAPTER 26 ~ THE LUCKY DRAGON BOOKSTORE

"Sally, do you think the mini meatballs should go before or after the little egg rolls?" Nora asked as she attempted to arrange snacks for the open house.

"Put the food in whatever order looks the best to you— I don't think it matters much," Sally said, knowing that most of their invited guests would be more interested in eating than eyeing the open house snacks.

People had been generous providing food; George, Nora's chef friend, had insisted that they serve miniature versions of his famous Gina's Italian Grill meatballs, and D'Wight had been equally insistent that they serve appetizer-sized egg rolls made from his mother's recipe.

The new bakery, just down the street from the store, had provided free cookies and bars as a thank you for being the exclusive wholesaler of baked goods to "Book Nook Coffee and Tea," the name Sally and Nora had settled on for the coffee area in the back corner of the bookstore. Sally had been fine with serving cookies at their open house, but she'd been worried about serving hot hors d'oeuvres in the pristine venue. Nora had told her to loosen up, saying, "It's a party, and it's mainly going to be our friends and fellow book lovers—they'll respect the books. If stuff gets on the floor, stuff gets on the floor— we've had lots of experience cleaning these floors over the past six months."

Sally finished arranging flowers in little colored-glass jars at the centers of the four small tables that graced the coffee nook and then called out to Nora, "It's time! Take off that apron so everyone can see your gorgeous dress." Nora had put her un-returnable wedding dress to good use by having it shortened and dyed. "Emerald green is definitely your color." Sally said as she walked toward the front windows. "Wow, looks like we have people waiting to get in. Are you ready?"

"I'm so ready," said Nora. "I think I've been waiting for this day my whole life."

Nora looked down at her dress and smoothed the skirt—it had been purchased for another day that she had been anticipating her whole life. A smile crossed her face at the thought. She looked around—this new adventure, even though it was just starting, was going to be so much better than being wed to Brad, a man who didn't understand her and probably never would have. The dress, now a lacy green confection, was the embodiment of luck. It was the dress that brought her to the Lucky Dragon in the first place—it was the reason she had met both D'Wight and Sally. While she'd been wrong about Brad, she'd been right about the dress all along. No matter its color or length, it was special.

Standing at the front door of The Lucky Dragon Bookstore, Sally turned the lock and threw off the deadbolt. The mechanical bell above the door bounced up and down, chiming gently as the first customers entered. Nora welcomed them into the new space that looked remarkably like it had when she'd first seen it during her encounters with the Lucky Dragon: polished wooden bookcases stretched floor to ceiling covering most of the walls; freestanding cases stood in rows toward the back of the room behind an L-shaped check-out counter; the front of the room held custom display tables covered with stacks of books, their replacements stored beneath; the left wall of the room, toward the front windows, featured a brick fireplace uncovered first by D'Wight's sledge hammer and further by the construction crew when they'd removed the old sheetrock; a wooden mantle stained the same color as the bookshelves surrounded the fireplace and comfy reading chairs flanked the hearth; and, in front of the sidewalk-facing windows, plants hung, their terracotta pots nestled in macramé hangers.

"Oh, this is just wonderful!" Dorothy cried.

"Indeed it is," added John, before asking where he might find books by his favorite author, Erik Larson. Nora had invited Dorothy and John to the open house the last time she'd seen them at Gina's—actually, the last night she'd worked at Gina's. She hadn't expected the elderly couple to come, let alone wait outside to be some of the store's first customers. *They are such kind people,* thought Nora.

All day long, friends and family dropped in to see Nora and Sally's labor-of-love. While Nora talked books, Sally showed people to the back of the store and invited them to enjoy treats and beverages. Today, below the hanging sign that read "Book Nook Coffee and Tea," she was serving punch, along with coffee and tea. In the future she planned to limit the selection of self-serve beverages to coffee, decaf, and an assortment of teas, including a Lapsang Souchong variety that she'd dubbed "Dragon's Breath." The mugs Sally had chosen for the coffee area were not the delicate bone china that the dragon had used when he'd prepared tea for her, but instead, sturdy white stoneware made by a company in St. Paul. They featured The Lucky Dragon Bookstore logo imprinted on raised medallions at their mid-sections. The logo was nearly the same design as the reconfigured neon sign now mounted on the white brick front of the building. It displayed a chubby dragon smoking a cigar. While the older restaurant version of the sign and logo had featured the dragon rolling dice—the new version showed the beast reading a book. Both the new logo and the revamped neon sign had been gifts from D'Wight.

Steps away from the coffee nook, in the children's section of the store, Melanie's daughter, Juliet, played contentedly with a plastic Curious George. Contentedly, that was, until Rosco and Ricco joined her and grabbed the little monkey from her hands. A piercing wail from the toddler brought Melanie, Trudy, and Nora running to her side from three different directions. "I'm so sorry," said Trudy to Melanie, and then said to the twins, "Give George back to the little girl. There are other toys you can play with."

Melanie spoke up when she saw the resemblance between Nora and Trudy. "Is this her?" she asked Nora.

"Yes," Nora chuckled, "How'd you guess?— Melanie I'd like you to meet my sister, Trudy, and nephews, Rosco and Ricco. We all met for the first time last night. Trudy, this is my long-time best friend, Melanie."

Trudy greeted Melanie and explained that her father, Bruce, had flown her and the twins back to Minnesota so that they could surprise Sally by attending the grand opening. "Dad's trying to get into Mom's good graces—I'm not sure that he wants to get back together, maybe, but I think he's mostly trying to make amends. I love my dad, but he's kinda. . . well, he's my dad. I don't think I'll say anything more. . ."

"Who's whose dad?" Jim asked as he walked up to Nora and put his arm around her.

"I was just introducing Melanie to Trudy, Dad," Nora said.

"You girls look so much alike to me," Jim said while shaking his head. "I find it amazing the way this has all played out. The coincidences involved in you two finding one another almost make a person believe in magic."

"And I always thought I looked just like Trudy," Tiffany said as she joined the group. "Mom sent me over here to ride herd on the play area." To the boys and Juliet, Tiffany asked in a sing-songy voice, "Who wants to hear a story?"

"We do! We do, An Tiffy," cried Rosco and Ricco in unison.

Juliet let go of Melanie's leg and, still clutching Curious George in her tiny hand, wandered over to Tiffany. She held George up toward the teen.

"Would you like to hear a story about George?" Tiffany asked. The boys shouted yes, and Juliet nodded as her mother and the other adults left to fill their plates.

"Are we too late to join story time?" came a high-pitched voice, nearly inaudible above the clicking of her

Manolo Blahniks as she raced toward Tiffany. It was Melanie's mom friend, Darcy, with her baby daughter, Violet, on her hip.

"No, you're welcome to join us as long as you *both* stay—your little girl seems a bit young to be unattended," Tiffany said.

"She's very mature for her age, but I can stay if it's store policy," Darcy said in a tone that conveyed both disappointment and dismay at being spoken to with authority by a teenager.

"I'm not sure the store has a policy, as yet. I just know that I've got my hands full with these two," Tiffany said while motioning with her head toward Rosco and Ricco.

"I see. Do you work here?" Darcy asked.

"No, I'm a volunteer today—although I might see if I can get a part-time job in a couple of weeks when I get my driver's license. I'm related to one of the owners—well, actually, both owners," Tiffany said.

"Nora?"

"Yeah, she's my half-sister, but at first I meant Sally—she's my mom."

"Ohhh. . . so your mother's the brains behind this beautiful store," Darcy said.

"I wouldn't say that—Mom's more like a silent partner. This is all Nora. Isn't it dope?—I mean, Nora's vision for this space was *estupendo*."

"Oh, it was. It really was—I am so proud to have her as a friend," Darcy said. Violet, still on her mother's hip, took that moment to spit up her punch and cookie all down Darcy's left side, even managing to douse one of her expensive shoes. "SHIT!" The loud expletive left Darcy's perfectly lipsticked lips before she realized what she was saying.

"She said SHIT!" cried Rosco. "STORY, NOW!" yelled Ricco, tired of waiting for his aunt to begin reading *Curious George.*

Tiffany, trying to hide her laughter, opened the book and began to read.

Darcy, head down, turned and slunk toward the restroom. Violet, still riding sidesaddle, screamed so loudly she could be heard in Wisconsin.

Deb and D'Wight stood in front of the checkout counter, staring at the huge paper dragon hanging from the ceiling. "Did you make this just for the store?" Nora's mother asked.

"No, originally I made it as an homage to the Lucky Dragon, my parent's—my—old restaurant, but I couldn't think of a better place for it than here in Nora's bookstore."

"Nora couldn't quit talking about it when you gave it to her," Deb said.

"I'm glad she likes it—I'm glad she likes origami. If she didn't, maybe none of this would have happened." D'Wight gestured around the store.

"What do you mean?—You lost me," Deb said.

"Okay, I'll see if I can put my thoughts into words." D'Wight paused. "Eight months ago, Nora walked into my restaurant. I hadn't opened for lunch yet, but she was hungry. . ."

"And, good looking," interjected Deb.

"Well, yes. . . anyway, I fed her egg rolls and helped her fold some cranes. Shortly after she left—about the time we officially opened for the day—Sally, who was a restaurant regular, walked in. She said something about me looking happy, and I told her I was smiling because I'd just met Nora. Anyway, the next time Nora was in the restaurant, Sally came in too, so I introduced them. . . Truthfully, I don't know how they became such good friends—it just seemed destined. And, then to find out that Sally is Nora's biological mother—that's just mind blowing."

"That's one way to describe it. Does everybody know? I thought Nora and Sally were going to keep things quiet," Deb said.

"I think they have—just family and close friends seem to know. Say, have you met Trudy—Nora's twin sister?" D'Wight asked.

"Yes, we all met last night at dinner. Of course, Jim and I already knew Sally. I was worried that it might be awkward meeting all of Nora's biological family, but it really wasn't. It was more like meeting long lost relatives—rather pleasant, except, well. . . Trudy's boys are a bit of a handful. Trudy seems nice, though."

"I'm sure she is—Sally raised her."

"What's that supposed to mean? You don't think Nora's nice?"

"No, Deb—I think your daughter is the nicest person in the world."

"If you're talking about Nora, I agree with you," remarked a tall woman carrying a book.

"And who are you?" Deb inquired in her normal brusque manner.

"I'm Barb. I work with—used to work with—Nora at Mill City Physical Therapy. It hasn't been nearly as much fun around the office since Nora left us."

D'Wight spoke up and held his hand out to Barb. "Hi, I'm D'Wight, and this is Nora's mom, Deb."

"It's nice to meet you. Nora talked about both of you." Barb said, grasping D'Wight's hand with her free right hand.

"She did?" D'Wight asked.

"Yes she did—all glowing comments. . . Do you know where Nora is? I'd like to pay for this book. I've been looking for a copy for ages—I could hardly believe it when I found it on the shelf of pre-owned books toward the back. It felt like magic," Barb said, holding up an almost pristine copy of the 1964 book, *Lark*, by Sally Watson.

As she pointed to the checkout counter, Deb said, "Just ring that desk bell—it's right beside that silly waving cat statue. Nora'll come running if she thinks she has a customer."

~

D'Wight's cat, Eggroll, lay curled on the back of one of the reading chairs by the fireplace. The little kitty had spent the open house begging for meatballs and affection. The long day had obviously worn her out. Nora locked the front door of the empty store and walked toward the back. "G'night, Eggroll," she said as she ran her hand over the prone feline from head to tail; then, turning and looking back at the store, Nora exhaled a long, satisfied sigh—she was looking at her dream come true. She finished walking to the back of the store, flipped the main floor light switches to OFF, and climbed the darkened winding staircase to share a celebratory nightcap with her new landlord.

CHAPTER 27 ~ NORA'S EPILOGUE

October 19, 2019

The sun shone down on a row of glorious autumn trees as Nora and D'Wight walked out of the courthouse, holding hands. D'Wight was wearing a gray suit and white shirt without a tie, and Nora had opted for a simple white dress that hugged her curves on top and flared at the waist. On her head sat a crown of white flowers woven with green foliage and gold ribbons. The surprise wedding had been D'Wight's idea. He had suggested since engagements appeared to be bad luck for Nora, they should just get married and throw a surprise party for their family and friends after the ceremony. Melanie and D'Wight's sister,

Iris, had served as witnesses and had been sworn to secrecy prior to the big day.

It had only been ten months since Nora and D'Wight's first date, but it had been the happiest ten months of Nora's life. With D'Wight, she didn't have to pretend to like sports or hoppy beers. She could count on him to attend parties and never worried that he wouldn't have her back. She loved his art and he loved her books. With D'Wight, she didn't have to be anyone but Nora.

The happy foursome piled into Melanie's SUV, and headed over to Gina's Italian Grill where their family and friends waited in the event space at the back of the restaurant for what the guests all assumed was an engagement party, not a wedding reception. "I can't wait to see everyone's faces," D'Wight said as he slid into the back seat next to Nora and grabbed her hand again. "This is going to be the best party ever." He kissed her cheek.

"It really is," Nora said, aglow with happiness.

Nora and D'Wight entered the back room of the restaurant to wild applause from their family and friends. The couple had come early that morning to decorate the space, and it was magical with floating paper cranes and bouquets of folded paper flowers atop each table. Mack, Gina's stalwart bartender, stood by the door with a tray set with two beautiful champagne flutes. Nora took a flute from the tray and handed it to D'Wight, then took the other for herself.

"Hey, Mack, I thought you'd be attending this shindig, not working it," she said. The bartender, out of his usual Gina's uniform of white shirt, black pants, and red bowtie and instead wearing khakis and a Hawaiian shirt, shrugged. "Can't help it—I guess serving's in my blood. Anyway, I had to make sure you were gettin' the good stuff. On the house, of course," he said as he winked.

Nora and D'Wight made their way to the table at the back of the room gathering hugs and handshakes along the way. Finally, arriving at their table, D'Wight picked up a knife and clinked the side of his glass, making the room fall silent. D'Wight raised his champagne flute. "When you know, you just know—I couldn't let this woman get away. Which is why this isn't an engagement party. . ." the crowd began to murmur, until D'Wight finished his declaration: "It's a wedding reception!" With those words, Nora and D'Wight held up their left hands, showing the matching silver bands that had been created by a jewelry artist in the Casket Arts building in exchange for one of D'Wight's origami assemblages.

The crowd burst into applause once again, whooping and whistling as D'Wight set down their champagne flutes and took Nora in his arms, dipping her back for a swoon-worthy kiss. After D'Wight set Nora back on her feet, he picked up and clinked his glass with the knife once again, this time to get the crowd to settle down. "Now, everyone go enjoy the buffet and open bar. We've got celebrating to do!"

While many folks followed directions, heading to the buffet tables full of giant meatballs, garlic bread, pastas and salads, Nora's parents approached the head table. "Well, it's not the wedding I expected for you, and I really would have preferred to be there for the vows," said Deb. "But. . . I'm happy for you, Nora. I've just always wanted to see you happy," she conceded.

"Thank you, Mom," Nora said, embracing Deb.

"Sweetheart, I'm just so happy for you," said Nora's dad after the two women let go of each other. He, then, scooped Nora into a bone-crushing hug. Jim had just finished a round of radiation thanks to Nora's insistence that he get a physical. The doctor said they'd caught the liver cancer very early, still stage one. The doctor also said that it was Nora's insistence that Jim get a complete blood panel that had likely saved his life.

After setting Nora back on her feet, Jim reached for D'Wight's hand, but then pulled him in for a hug as well. "Thank you for making my little girl so happy, D'Wight. Welcome to the family."

"Thank you, Mr. Wanamaker," D'Wight said, sounding a bit breathless following Jim's bearhug.

"Please call me Jim. Or Dad—Dad works too," Jim said.

Sally, champagne glass in hand, approached the bride and groom as Jim and Deb walked away. "Well, I guess I can sort of welcome you into the family, too, D'Wight," said Sally. "It's odd—I feel like I've been part of your lives together since the day you and Nora met. Maybe we never know what makes two people into a couple, but in your and Nora's case, I think we can credit fate."

"And a wedding gown—just not this one," Nora said as she gestured toward her simple white dress.

"And origami," D'Wight countered as he refilled their champagne flutes.

"And the Lucky Dragon," added Sally, "don't forget the Lucky Dragon." Sally lifted her glass into the air. "Here's to the Lucky Dragon!"

"To the Lucky Dragon!" Nora and D'Wight responded as they clinked their glasses with Sally's.

CHAPTER 28 ~ SALLY'S EPILOGUE

November 16, 2019

"Ms. Johnson plays with the vigor of youth, yet with an emotional maturity gained only through a lifetime of experiences. In her music, her audiences hear great joy, as well as the fury of anger and the pathos of unimaginable sorrow. Her impassioned playing is a gift to the world."

Bertram Libby, *Minneapolis Star Tribune*

Professional recognition had exploded following a human-interest story that appeared in the *Star Tribune* about Sally's reacquired piano skills. Small concerts—at first, booked out of curiosity or pity, and later because of rave reviews—had led to an invitation to perform for the Schubert Club at the Ordway Center. Sally's regained prowess at the keyboard after such a long hiatus was making her a classical music star in the Midwest and, perhaps, after this evening's scheduled concert, the whole of North America.

Arriving at the concert hall, Sally was greeted by a poster. It was the same image that had run in Twin Cities' newspapers and been plastered over billboards along I-94. SARA JOHNSON — A RE-RISING STAR. The poster featured a toned Sally sitting at a Steinway grand, holding a porcelain cup of steaming tea, and smiling as though nothing had ever gone wrong in her entire life.

Sally entered the greenroom. She had requested that nothing be furnished to her except several bottles of water, so she was surprised to see three bouquets. She opened the little envelope attached to the smallest of them. The card read: "Mommy, wish we could be with you on your big night, but considering your grandsons' behavior these days, you're lucky we're in Maryland. Break a leg! Love, Trudy, Enrique, Rosco, and Ricco." The second bouquet, an arrangement featuring two-toned gladiolas, was from the Schubert Club. *Nice,* thought Sally, *but totally unnecessary—they're paying me.* The last bouquet, two dozen long-stemmed red roses, was the most intriguing. The card with the roses read: "Dear Sara, Please meet me here after your performance tonight. Always, Your Biggest Fan." Sally put the card down. *Who would make such a gesture? Bruce? Nah, he would never call me Sara, and even though he seems to want me to forgive him, he wouldn't buy me two dozen of anything. But who else could it be—maybe one of my former piano teachers is still living? Ehh, later, I'll figure it out later. . .*

After standing ovations and two encores, Sally returned to the greenroom. She flopped on the stiff plastic couch as happy as she'd been since Lucky D had granted her the wish that had reunited her with her piano virtuosity. She closed her eyes and smiled in satisfaction. Tiffany, Nora, and D'Wight would soon be at the door to escort her to the post-concert party across Rice Park at The Saint Paul Hotel. She'd been a bit miffed when she'd first heard the Schubert Club's choice of party venue, but realized that it was silly to blame the elegant hotel for Bruce's affair. *And, what the hell—"all's well that ends well," as Lucky D would have said.* When she heard a knock at the door, Sally opened her eyes.

"Hello, Sally," came the low melodic voice that Sally had thought she would never hear again. Bentley B. Bradley stood in the doorway, his slim, fifty-six-year-old frame bent slightly to one side. He held a cane in his right hand and his face was dominated by an old scar that traveled the length of his left cheek, but other than those physical details, Ben showed no signs of having been dead for over thirty-five years. He was tanned and as handsome as he had ever been; his still thick black hair was now salt-and-pepper, but the love beaming from his eyes hadn't changed.

Sally stood, mouth agape, and walked toward Ben, her arms outstretched. They hugged until Sally dropped her arms and stepped back to look at Ben. "I—I. . . thought you were dead," she stammered, tears of joy running down her cheeks.

"Obviously, you were wrong," Ben countered with a smile as big as Sally's. "At first, I thought you were gone, too. My mother told me that you and our baby had died in the accident. I found out years later that you were alive, but by then you were married, and I didn't want to disrupt your life. When I happened to read an AP story in my local paper, and the reporter mentioned that you were divorced, well, I knew I had to come see you—hear you. . ."

The couple embraced again and were still in each other's arms when Tiffany, Nora, and D'Wight knocked at the open greenroom door. Sally, who had just minutes earlier been expecting their arrival, was now startled by the knock.

"Mom, you were terrific! —and it looks like someone else thought so, too," Tiffany said, eyeing Ben with a questioning stare.

"Yes, she was," said Ben. "She's as good as she ever was—better, even!"

Sally spoke up. "I'd like you guys to meet an old friend of mine. This is Bentley Bradley." Gesturing toward each young adult, Sally continued, "Ben, this is my daughter Tiffany Munson; my good friend and landlord, D'Wight Wong; and this young woman—who has what I now realize are your eyes—is Nora Wanamaker-Wong. She's one of *your* twin daughters. Your other daughter, Trudy, and your twin grandsons live in Maryland."

After Ben regained his ability to speak, and, followed by a rush of asked and answered questions, the group of five walked across the park to join the post-concert party already in full swing at The Saint Paul Hotel.

As they'd left the Ordway greenroom, Sally could have sworn she smelled Lucky D's cigar smoke wafting through the corridor.

ACKNOWLEDGEMENTS

Samantha MacDonald Solberg

It's hard to believe you're holding a finished book that I helped write in your hands, my wonderful, beautiful reader. First and foremost, I have my mother, Beth MacDonald, to thank for that. I'm so grateful she took a chance on co-writing with me—not to mention putting up with me taking forever to finish Nora's chapters. Thank you so much to my friends, affectionately known as the Smols, for taking on the task of being beta readers of this novel and providing feedback: Carolyn Anderson, Kyra Berkness D'Aloia, Andrew Bruski, Fallon Moore, Sarah Mosier, and Meagan Weber. Thanks to my brother-in-law, Garrick Solberg, who volunteered several years ago to be a beta reader when he found out I was writing a book and followed through on his promise. Also, thank you to our final beta reader, Lindsay Pluger, for the support and wise feedback about adoption. Finally, thank you to my husband, Collin Solberg, for always supporting my dreams.

Beth MacDonald

A huge thank you to those of you who have helped me with my third novel! My first acknowledgment goes to my daughter, Samantha Solberg, who, when I explained the premise of the book I was thinking about writing, said, "If I saw that book at a bookstore, I'd buy it." When I responded by asking her to help me write the book, with no hesitation she said, "Yes!" Without Sam as my co-author, I doubt that you would be holding *The Lucky Dragon* in your hands today; My second shout-out goes to the wonderful novelist, Ellen Baker. Ellen read our first draft and gave thoughtful and constructive suggestions on how to make *The Lucky Dragon* a better experience for our readers. Next, I need to thank my very first beta reader—a friend since junior high— Debbie Nelson Sandhurst. Debbie spent hours analyzing our characters and giving us valuable feedback. Our next beta readers were the members of my multi-generational book club in Sioux Falls, South Dakota. These wonderful women have served as my earliest readers and cheerleaders throughout the creation of three novels. They are: Julie Breu, Melissa Godber, LaVonne Hardy, Carolyn Johnson, Laurie Megard, Deanna Parker, Barb Roehrich, Angie Sewell, and, although they aren't with us any longer, the hilarious Charl Wendt and the unforgettable Dianna Hummel. And, my final thank you goes to the remarkably gifted, Romy Klessen, who once again worked her magic on the computer to make *The Lucky Dragon* look so darn good!

ABOUT THE AUTHORS

Samantha MacDonald Solberg has been creating stories on paper since childhood. In her day job, she flexes this muscle as a communications and marketing professional. For over 15 years, she's written stories, worked with the media, and built audiences on behalf of mission-driven organizations. When not writing, Samantha can usually be found watching soccer with friends or hanging out with her husband Collin, cat Cece, and basset hound Dixie in their Minneapolis, MN, home. *The Lucky Dragon* is her first published novel.

Beth MacDonald, a former professional craft designer, is the author of two previous novels, *A History of Forever* and *And One Other*, and a book of poetry, *Twenty-five: A Memoir of Cancer*. She has been a resident of Minneapolis, MN, since 2017, but spends most summer weekends at her longtime lake cabin in South Dakota and escapes the cold Minnesota winters in a quirky cottage in Beaufort, SC.

To learn more about Samantha and Beth, please visit www.NorthInkBooks.com